'Why are you so determined to destroy Brett Hilliard?'

'I'm not!' Rebecca denied hotly. 'It's nothing personal.'

'Well, that's a relief,' said a husky voice over her shoulder. She shivered a little. So Brett had come, had he? Well, she didn't mind defending her feelings to his face.

'It's just that I've seen this sort of project before, right here in Fultonsville. Why should we trust his word? I'm not exactly against the project . . .'

'You certainly do a good imitation of it,' said Brett Hiliard smoothly.

She jumped up, anxious to get away from him. 'If I make one person here think hard enough to start asking tough questions, I'll have accomplished my purpose.' She went into the house, and didn't stop until she reached the conservatory. 'At least they can't say they weren't warned,' she said aloud.

'You can't blame them for not liking the warning.' The deep voice, soft as it was, filled the space and seemed to make the glass panels vibrate. 'You did choose an abrasively public way of making your point.'

REBEL WITH A CAUSE

BY

LEIGH MICHAELS

MILLS & BOON LIMITED
ETON HOUSE   18–24   PARADISE ROAD
RICHMOND   SURREY   TW9 1SR

First published in Great Britain 1987 by Mills & Boon Limited

© Leigh Michaels 1987

Australian copyright 1987 Philippine copyright 1987 This edition 1987

ISBN 0 263 75792 7

Set in Times 10 on 10½ pt. 01-1087-54463

Computer typeset by SB Datagraphics, Colchester, Essex

Printed and bound in Great Britain by Collins, Glasgow

CHAPTER ONE

THE iron fire-escape rattled alarmingly under her feet as she ran up the steps and fumbled for her key to the private back door of the Broadcast Building. Traffic had been heavy this morning, and—as usual—Rebecca Barclay was cutting her schedule right to the minute. As a result, she thought, she would probably be on Jack Barnes's list of least favourite people again . . .

Of course, to be perfectly honest, she had to admit that in the four years she had worked for the small radio and television station which served Fultonsville she had seldom managed to stay on the programme director's good side for more than a day at a time. Fortunately for me, she told herself lightly, my listeners adore me, and they would picket the station if he tried to take me off the air.

The back door opened on to a shallow hallway, which at the moment was deserted. She tiptoed past the open door of the television studio, where Jack was probably lurking, waiting for her to show up. She ducked down the hall to her own tiny office.

Rebecca was convinced that the windowless room had once been a cupboard. Now it was fitted up with a swivel chair, a tiny table, and a telephone, and there was hardly room left for her. It was an inadequate arrangement for the hostess of the popular afternoon radio show, *Rebel with a Cause*.

'The next chance I get,' Rebecca said aloud, looking around with irritation at the cramped quarters, 'I am going to demand a bigger office.'

'I wouldn't do it today,' a woman's voice recommended. 'Jack's been pacing the broadcast studio and chain-smoking all morning, waiting for you to show up.'

Rebecca glanced at her wristwatch. 'He said he wanted to tape the TV show at ten, Janet,' she said, with a shrug of her shoulders. 'It's still five minutes till.'

The receptionist shook her head. 'All I know is that he's furious. Here are your messages—I expected you'd be sneaking in the back way.'

Rebecca tossed the stack of memos aside and returned to the attack. 'This office is ridiculous,' she said. 'It's bad enough when I bring a guest here before a show starts. There's no place for anyone to sit. But if Jack is going to expect me to keep filling in on the television side, he's just going to have to give me a larger office. I need a dressing-table, at least.' She grabbed a hair brush and bent over, brushing her long auburn hair against the grain as if she was about to wrap it into a bun atop her head. When she straightened up and shook her head, the wavy locks fell naturally into place about her shoulders. A quick touch of the brush here and there smoothed the loose hairs, leaving her looking natural and casual.

Janet shook her head admiringly. 'I never have understood how you do that.'

'I was born lucky.' Rebecca peered into the tiny mirror on the back of the office door. 'Damn these freckles,' she muttered and dashed powder across her nose.

'It will take all the luck you possess to get out of that studio in one piece this morning.'

'I can handle Jack Barnes any day of the year.'

'The guest you're interviewing might be a different story. He's been in the green room waiting for you for half an hour.'

Rebecca said indistinctly as she reapplied lipstick, 'That is his problem.'

Janet grunted. 'Well, it might be yours, too. He didn't look pleased at being kept kicking his heels because you're late.'

'I am never late. I'm just never early, because it's a

waste of time.' She smiled triumphantly, settled her dark blue linen jacket smoothly across her shoulders. 'Oh, by the way——' She waved her left hand under Janet's nose.

'Oh, my gosh!' Janet seized her fingers and studied the sparkling diamond solitaire set in the simple gold band. 'I didn't think Paul would ever come through. When did he propose?'

'Last night.' Rebecca wished that Janet hadn't said it quite that way; she made it sound as if Rebecca had been stalking the man!

'Has he told his parents?'

Rebecca didn't quite care for the sound of that either. 'Of course he told them. It wouldn't be decent not to.'

'And is Mama in favour?'

Rebecca shrugged. 'She seems quite happy about it. I haven't told my father yet, though.'

'And you're wearing that ring here?'

'So who's going to see it? The show won't be broadcast till tonight, and I'll tell him before then. Paul and I are going there for dinner. I've got to get on to the set, Janet.' She walked down the hall and arrived in the television studio just as the sweep second-hand of the big clock on the wall crossed the hour.

A balding man with a cigarette in his hand was standing in the centre of the room, shaking a finger at one of the cameramen. Rebecca watched him thoughtfully for a moment, and then smiled. The other cameraman had seen her; she silenced him with a finger over her lips and walked slowly across the room till she was within a foot of the programme director, who was still absorbed in his lecture.

'Good morning, Jack,' she said cheerfully. 'Let's get this show out of the way, shall we?'

The balding man wheeled around. 'Rebel, you have kept a crew waiting for the last time——'

'You said ten o'clock,' she reminded him crisply. 'It's ten, I won't remind you that filling in for Len Wilson

when he's on vacation isn't listed in my job description—
and I don't get paid for it.'

'You could have come in a little early to meet your
guests,' he pointed out.

'I've done my research. I prefer not to form im-
pressions of the people I interview before the show
starts; it makes it more interesting that way. If you're
worried about the show, Jack,' she added sweetly, 'let me
assure you, it will be dynamite.'

She walked across to the door of the green room, the
small reception area where guests awaited their turns to
appear on the station's shows. 'Mr Hilliard, we're ready
for you now.'

She didn't pause to study the man who was standing at
the window, his back to her, his jacket pushed back and
hands thrust deep in his trouser pockets. She had the
fleeting impression that he was furious, but that was no
more than she expected. No doubt, Jack, familiar with
private citizens who had little understanding of how
important it was to be on time in the broadcast business,
had told him to come in early. Actually, she felt a little
sorry for Brett Hilliard. If he was furious going into the
show, she would bet that he would be livid by the time it
was over.

She swallowed a little smile. In a controversial
situation, an angry guest was the best kind. He was far
more likely to slip up, to say things he hadn't meant to
confide. And that made the sort of show that Rebecca
liked best.

She settled herself in the upholstered chair and clipped
the tiny microphone to her jacket lapel. The technician
was working on Brett Hilliard, arranging his microphone. She let her eyes rest on him for a moment,
summing him up. She had read a lot about her guest, but
this was the first time she had ever seen him in the flesh.

And there wasn't a spare ounce of it anywhere on him
either, she thought with reluctant admiration. He must

be at least two inches over six feet; she was tall herself, but she'd had the impression in the green room that he towered above her. Under the strong television lights, his hair gleamed blue-black. He was wearing a dark blue suit, a yellow shirt, a neatly striped tie. Somebody had told him how to dress for television, she thought, and straightened the yellow silk scarf at her own throat.

We must look like a matched pair in our blue and yellow, she thought, and fought down the giggles. It was silly, after four years of live radio, to get a case of stage-fright over a television show that was to be videotaped for later use. But she always did; there was something about having a permanent record of what she had said that bothered her. As soon as the red camera light went on she would be fine. She always was.

'Test your mike, Rebel,' the technician said.

Automatically, she began, 'The owl and the pussycat went to sea, in a beautiful pea-green boat. They took some honey, and plenty of money, wrapped up in——'

'Why you can't just say the alphabet or something beats me,' the technician grumbled.

Rebecca smiled. 'Because it wouldn't give you a full range of my voice, that's why. Besides, this is the only exposure to poetry that you guys ever——'

'Good enough. Mr Hilliard, would you count to ten for me?'

He did, in the most gorgeous baritone Rebecca had ever heard. It reminded her vaguely of a pipe-organ she had once heard, being played by a master hand. She shook her head a little. Good grief, she told herself. So the man sounded as if he could play God in any Hollywood extravaganza. If anything, that should make her even more suspicious of him. A man with a voice like that could sell mink coats in Tahiti——

'We're on a tight schedule this morning,' Jack Barnes was saying. 'We'll have to be out of the studio in an hour. The sales unit was very co-operative, but we are interrupting their work. And since this is to be broadcast tonight, there isn't going to be time to do anything over. So we'll have to shoot the show just as though we were going on the air live.'

Rebecca sighed. She hated live television, but in a station this size, with only one studio, compromises had to be made. At least, she thought, on the radio side of the operation, there were plenty of broadcast booths. If she was trying to air *Rebel with a Cause* from her office, there wouldn't be room for her with all the equipment, much less a guest!

'I'll be cueing you from the control-booth, Rebel,' Jack went on, 'because I'll be doing the editing while we tape. With this late start, it's the only way we can have the show finished for air time tonight. There will be two station breaks. All ready?'

She nodded, ignoring his glare, and settled herself more comfortably in the upholstered chair.

'You forgot your notes,' Jack pointed out.

'I don't need any.'

The programme director looked less than pleased, but he didn't argue. He retreated to the glass-walled control-booth, and a moment later she heard the muffled sounds of the theme music for *Talk of the Town*. She used the one minute of credits to study Brett Hilliard covertly. He looked relaxed, at ease, in the big chair. His fury seemed to have vanished, to be replaced with something that looked like boredom. Another unprepared interviewer, he seemed to be thinking. Obviously, Rebecca thought, he's done this sort of thing before. He thinks I'm just another small-town hick, impressed by his big-city charm.

And, she decided, Rebecca Barclay—Rebel to her listeners—had better mind her own business, and stop speculating on what colour Mr Hilliard would turn when he discovered that she was far from unprepared. Remember, Rebecca, she told herself, that though it's a bright summer morning outside, this tape will be shown at night. If you forget it, Jack Barnes will have your head.

The red light blinked to life atop camera number one, and she smiled into it. 'Good evening, and welcome to *Talk of the Town*,' she said. 'I'm Rebel Barclay, sitting in for Len Wilson, who's on vacation this week. My guest tonight is Brett Hilliard, president of Hilliard Confectioners, the manufacturers of one of the most expensive lines of luxury chocolates on the market. Welcome, Mr Hilliard.'

He nodded, smiled. 'Thank you, Miss Barclay. I must say it's a pleasure to be able to talk to you at last.'

It was smooth, innocuous. Rebel's eyes sharpened, but there was nothing but innocence in his expression. 'Mr Hilliard, you have been talking to the Fultonsville City Council for the last several weeks about the question of building a new factory in the industrial park here, a plant that would become the main producer of Hilliard chocolates in the nation.'

'That's right.' He didn't enlarge on the subject, and for a moment, Rebel's heart sank. Did Brett Hilliard know that the best way to sabotage a broadcast was to refuse to answer questions fully? He wouldn't dare do it, she told herself. It's to his advantage to make a good impression on this show, and he can't do that by confining himself to Yes and No answers.

She smiled at him. 'You certainly don't look as though you over-indulge in your product,' she said, purposely inviting a laugh. Would he admit to a dislike of the stuff, she wondered.

'I grew up around chocolate,' he said, 'as a member of an old candy-making family. The Hilliards have been in the confectionery business for three hundred years, in one way or another. While other parents were warning their children not to eat too much candy, my father was handing me a new combination and asking what I thought of it.'

'And what is your favourite?' Rebecca asked. Her voice was a throaty purr.

'I can't tell a lie,' he confided. 'I always pick the caramels out of the box first. Always have, since I was a kid.'

Out of the corner of her eye, she could see Jack Barnes in the control-room. He looked slightly ill, as if he was wondering how an award-winning public affairs programme like *Talk of the Town* had suddenly degenerated into mindless babble. She wanted to tell him that she knew exactly what she was doing, that as soon as Brett Hilliard relaxed a little she would move in for the kill.

'They're my favourite, too,' she said.

'I find it interesting,' he went on, 'that most people say caramels are their favourites, and yet cream centres and liqueurs are actually our better sellers.'

Enough of this, Rebecca thought. The subject is not only sticky and sweet, it's becoming nauseating. But it's serving the purpose of getting him off guard. 'What draws you to Fultonsville?' she asked.

He had relaxed somewhat, and was sitting with his elbows on the arms of his chair, his fingers clasped. On his right hand he wore a heavy gold signet ring. 'My real estate man says the three most important things to look for when buying property are location, location and location,' he said.

'That's interesting.'

'Fultonsville, because of its position on the Mississippi River, is uniquely well situated for a company like ours that imports so much of its raw material. We could ship cacao beans up the river by barge, and cut our delivery time in half. The rest of our raw materials will be just as easy to ship. And as for the dairy products for our milk chocolates, we've always prided ourselves on using the freshest possible ingredients. You can't get much fresher than having a dairy farm right down the road.'

'I'm sure that will be a great help,' Rebecca murmured.

'Your firm is presently located in Chicago, am I correct?'

'On the outskirts.'

'And your reason for wanting to move?'

'We've been in our present location for seventy years. In that time, the city has grown up around us, and left us, unfortunately, without room to expand. The demand for Hilliard chocolates exceeds the supply, and we need new equipment, more workers, and a bigger plant to meet our customers' needs.'

'And you've chosen Fultonsville because of its river location?'

'Fultonsville is one of the locations we're looking at,' he corrected. 'Our employees are impressed with the town as well. They like the idea of getting out of the city, of raising families in a town with good schools, pleasant parks, and affordable housing. And of course, our employees are like family members at Hilliard. They own part of the company, so we listen to what they say.'

This is almost it, she thought. He had very nearly taken the bait. But before she could phrase her next question, she saw that in the control-booth, Jack Barnes had raised a hand to indicate it was time for a commercial break. Just as well, she thought. This way it would hit him even harder when she began asking her really tough questions. Rebecca turned towards the camera. 'We'll be back in a minute to hear more from our guest, Brett Hilliard.'

The lights went off, and she wriggled in her chair. Brett Hilliard didn't move. 'Barclay,' he said thoughtfully. 'The Mayor's named Barclay.'

'That's right,' Rebecca said crisply. She kicked at a cable that snaked under her chair.

'Is he any relation to you?'

As often as she had been asked that question, Rebecca thought, she should have come up with a snappy answer for it by now. But no matter; today the truth would work better than anything else possibly could. 'His Honour is my esteemed father.'

Brett Hilliard seemed to relax. 'He's been very helpful
in getting information for us, you know. It's encouraging
to find civic officials so excited about the possibility of
new industry that they're willing to do anything in their
power to help.'

She smiled at him. In the control-room, Jack signalled
that the pause was coming to an end. 'I know,' she
purred. 'That's precisely why I think he's being an idiot
on this issue.'

The camera focused on him was not the one that went
live at that instant; Rebecca thought mournfully that she
would always regret the fact that Brett Hilliard's
expression was not transmitted for the benefit of the
viewers.

She resumed the broadcast, smoothly. 'We're talking
to Brett Hilliard about the possibility that his company
may be making Fultonsville its home in the near future.
Mr Hilliard, you were telling me a few moments ago
about what makes Fultonsville attractive to your
company. But you didn't say anything about the package
of financial incentives that the Mayor and City Council
have put together to encourage this move.'

'You haven't given me an opportunity,' he said quietly.

Rebecca ignored him. 'As I understand it,' she said,
'the financial investment that the taxpayers of Fultonsville will be making, if Hilliard Confectioners comes to
town, will be more than eleven million dollars. Now
really, Mr Hilliard, don't you think that sounds a little
excessive?'

He hadn't moved, hadn't stirred in his chair. Why,
then, did she get the feeling that the relaxed charm had
been replaced by a steel spring, coiled tight and ready to
leap at her?

'Yes, I'd call it excessive. I don't know where you got
that figure, Miss Barclay——'

'From our competition,' she admitted cheerfully. 'I

read it in the Fultonsville *Chronicle*.'

'——but it's not accurate. The proposal made by the City Council includes land already owned by the city, a shell building to be constructed at Council expense, and concessions on property taxes and other operating costs.'

'I understand the utility companies have agreed to give you all the electricity and natural gas you need for the first year,' Rebecca inserted neatly.

'That's true. But the total figure does not come nearly as high as you state. The true total for land, building and concession will be somewhere in the neighbourhood of five to six million dollars.'

He had done it; he had stepped neatly into her trap. Rebecca tried to hide her smile, and said, smoothly, 'So what you're saying, Mr Hilliard, is that you're asking the taxpayers of Fultonsville to kick in six million dollars to subsidise your company—which last year, according to your stockholder reports, made a tidy pre-tax profit—so that you can move from a highly industrialised area, sell your plant there to the highest bidder, and come here. I understand there is a great deal of interest in your Chicago location——'

'Selling the Chicago plant is one of several options we're looking at.' His voice was quiet; his eyes had gone cold as steel. 'I think you've done some very one-sided research, Miss Barclay. The City Council is obviously in no doubt about the benefits to Fultonsville if the company relocates here, or they wouldn't have made this very generous offer. And by the way, they did offer; I didn't go to them and make demands.'

'I'm sure you're a much smoother operator than that, Mr Hilliard.'

He ignored the interruption. 'This county is suffering from the highest unemployment rate in the state. Your elected officials saw a chance to do something about that. When Hilliard Confectioners moves—and it will move, Miss Barclay; that decision was made a year ago—we plan to hire at least five hundred new workers over the next three years.'

'How do we know you'll carry through with that promise?'

He paid no attention. 'The City Council has very wisely asked—and we have agreed to the condition—that if we move here, we will hire our new workers from among those who are currently unemployed. Not only will that remove those five hundred families from the welfare rolls, it will give them an income to spend in Fultonsville's retail area. Those people will buy everything from running-shoes to homes. They will be paying property taxes and income taxes, and the money they spend will hire additional workers in stores and support businesses. It's called a multiplying factor, Miss Barclay—or didn't you study basic economics in school?'

Rebecca leaned back in her chair. Despite her best intentions of ignoring any sarcastic comments uttered by an angry guest—especially one whom she had badgered into fighting—his words had stung a little. 'My goodness, Mr Hilliard,' she said softly, 'let's not get personal here. I certainly meant nothing against you; I'm sure you intend to keep your promises.' She turned towards the camera. 'Do stay with us; we'll continue our discussion in just a minute.'

The lights blinked out. 'That,' Brett Hilliard said, 'was a low blow.'

She readjusted her microphone, fussing with the lapel of her jacket. 'I'm a reporter, Mr Hilliard. I am not a public relations campaign for Hilliard chocolates.'

'My God, at least be fair about it——'

'I'll have to ask you to watch your language when we go back on the air.'

'You should have a complaint filed against you. Freedom of the press is one thing, but this sort of railroading——'

Jack Barnes went through his motions in the control-room. Rebecca smiled at the camera, ignoring the furious man beside her. 'We're back with Brett Hilliard, discussing the economic package that the City Council has offered to Hilliard Confectioners. Mr Hilliard, I would just like to ask why you think that the taxpayers of Fultonsville should pay the bill for your new plant, your move, your utility costs——'

'And I've pointed out, Miss Barclay, that the community stands to gain three to five dollars of benefits for every dollar spent. You've also conveniently forgotten that the company will be paying rent. If we choose to come here——' his eyes, cold and hard, seemed to say that at the moment he couldn't think of a single reason why he would agree to do that '—we will sign a long-term lease. The payments start out low and increase every year, so that by the end of the ten-year lease, the city will have been repaid for every cent it has spent on the land and the building. At that time, we will take over ownership of the building, we will be paying full property taxes, we will be buying electricity and natural gas——'

'Will you pay any interest on the loan advanced by the city?'

'Not as such, but the increased employment over the long term——'

'What if there isn't a long term? What if you decide in three years that it was a mistake to move to Fultonsville?'

'We would have an unbreakable lease,' he said stiffly.

Rebecca shrugged. 'That's no big deal. You could pay off the lease from petty cash. If you close the plant, you won't even have utility costs. What guarantee does Fultonsville have that after we spend all this money to bring you here, you'll stay?'

'We've been in our present location for seventy——'

'I know; you told me. But that, Mr Hilliard,' she smiled sweetly, 'was in a different age, and under different management. What if, in five years when the costs start to get high, Hilliard Confectioners starts

looking around for another city willing to offer economic
concessions and put up a building to house your
business? What guarantee do we have that this project
won't become a gigantic Fultonsville's Folly?'

'You have a poetic soul, Miss Barclay,' he said mildly.
'I could almost believe that you planned your whole line
of questioning to end up with that allusion. But you seem
to have forgotten that the original Fulton's Folly—the
steamship—turned out to be a huge commercial success,
despite the laughter of its critics.' He shook his head
sadly. 'You apparently make a habit of not doing your
research. By the way, Miss Barclay, where did you buy
that jacket you're wearing?'

'We are not discussing clothing here; we're talking
about chocolates and economic incentives for
industry——'

'Just indulge me and answer my question.' He was
smiling, and the warmth was back in his voice. She had
been right about her instinctive assessment of his charm;
she could feel it oozing over her. She knew there was a
trap yawning before her, but for the life of her she
couldn't recognise it. Time was running out, and she
obviously had to get off the defensive. 'In St Louis, at
Laclede's Landing. Why do you ask?'

'Did you buy it there because there was nothing of the
sort available in Fultonsville? And why wasn't there,
Miss Barclay? Shops don't support themselves, you
know. There has to be a payroll in the town, or no one can
afford to buy the merchandise. Don't you think that
another industry in Fultonsville might encourage the
merchants to stock additional colours and sizes and
styles? Hilliard Confectioners will be bringing a couple
of hundred new families to town, if we come here. Add to
that the fact that we'll be hiring more people, ones who
already live here but who haven't been able to buy what
they want. Your station might even benefit,' he added
gently. 'Those retail stores will have to find a way to let

everyone know about their new merchandise, won't they? Perhaps they'll buy advertising time.'

From the corner of her eye, Rebecca could see Jack Barnes making the circling gesture that indicated sixty seconds of air time left.

'Mr Hilliard,' she said briskly, 'we're coming to the close of our programme, and we've barely scratched the surface. I know you're only in town for a short trip this time, but perhaps next time you come, you could fit in an appearance on *Rebel with a Cause*, to discuss it further?'

He leaned back in his chair, as if thinking about it. Part of her hoped that he would refuse; he would be the one who looked a fool if he declined. And yet—it had been a very neat attempt to turn the tables on her. Something told her he wasn't the kind to accept defeat easily.

'I'd be delighted, Miss Barclay. But are you certain you want to explore the topic quite so publicly? We could have dinner together instead and discuss it—it might save you some embarrassment.'

She ignored him, with an effort. 'Our guest tonight has been Brett Hilliard, and we've been discussing the prospective move of Hilliard Confectioners to Fultons-ville. Join Len Wilson and his guest next week on *Talk of the Town*.'

Jack Barnes made a throat-cutting signal; the camera lights died, and Rebecca sank down in her chair. But only for a moment. 'I'd appreciate it if you stuck to the issues, Mr Hilliard,' she said. 'It's none of your business whether I'm embarrassed or not.' She turned to Jack. 'Edit that last remark of his out of the tape, Jack.'

Brett Hilliard shrugged. 'As a gentleman, I hate to see a lady make a fool of herself in public. But since you're determined, I can't stop you.'

'Even you must admit that there are two sides to this issue.'

'That's correct. There's the right side, and then there is

your side. I'll be back next week for the council meeting if you were serious about your offer. Do you want to tangle over this matter again?'

She felt just a little breathless, but there was no backing down now. 'Wednesday?'

'Fine with me.'

'One-thirty in the afternoon. It's a two-hour talk show with telephone calls from the public.'

'I'll be there. But let me warn you, Miss Barclay——'

'Yes?'

'If you want to play games, like two street cats, just remember—I didn't scratch first, but I can scratch hard.'

He didn't look back as he crossed the studio.

CHAPTER TWO

REBECCA'S apartment, on the first floor of an old Victorian house, was hot when she came home late that afternoon. She thought about turning on the air-conditioning, but rejected the idea as impractical. By the time the apartment was cool, Paul would be there to pick her up for the barbecue at her father's house. So she took a quick shower, put on a bare-shouldered gingham sun-dress and sandals, and went to sit on the front porch steps where there was a breeze.

The gingerbread-laden house had once been a man-sion, built by a grocery wholesaler who had made his fortune before the turn of the century, when Fultonsville was a thriving river town. Now, after a period of disuse and decay, the house had been restored and cut into apartments. Rebecca's part was the front half of the first floor, what had once been the master bedroom, sitting-room, and nursery. It was small, but it was sunny and bright and the tiny kitchen and bathroom were brand new. The heating system was efficient, the water always hot, and the location good. It suited Rebecca just fine. She especially liked her living-room, which had an octagonal tower room extending off one corner. She loved to sit there in the window-seat in the winter, drinking hot chocolate and watching the snow fall . . .

Chocolate. The mere word brought Brett Hilliard's face to her mind. He was an arrogant chauvinist, she thought irritably. The nerve of him, to say that there were two points of view about the factory's move—hers, and the right one! All she had done was to express a decided difference of opinion. She only wanted to stimulate some discussion of this new project—so far, it

seemed to her, everyone in Fultonsville was falling neatly
into line, saying, 'Yes, isn't this a wonderful idea?'
without ever considering the possibility that it might all
fall through and leave the city with a horrendous debt to
pay off, without a single additional job, and with another
huge empty building in the industrial park. It was
obvious that Brett Hilliard would have preferred to talk
about chocolate and Rebecca's poetic soul rather than to
get down to issues.

'Well, he's going to discuss the issues,' she said firmly.
'If I'm the only one who's willing to get down in the mud
with him, then that's the way it will have to be.
Somebody has to do it, for the sake of the town.'

It was, after all, her job. In a town the size of
Fultonsville, Rebecca had learned, the press too often
acted as a sort of extension of the Chamber of
Commerce, publishing only the good news. But Rebecca
was different. Her years in journalism school at the
university had taught her to feel the full weight of the
public trust that had been lodged in her as a representa-
tive of the people. A good reporter, she felt, had to be
above personalities, willing to ask the tough questions
and seek out the truth, no matter who might be hurt in
the search.

I wish that everyone could just understand that I've
got nothing personal against Brett Hilliard, she told
herself. I've said worse things about my own father,
when I thought he was dodging questions!

Paul's car, a dark grey medium sized sedan, pulled up
at the front gate. She started towards it, and was not
surprised when he got out and came around to open her
door. It was one of the things she liked best about Paul,
she decided. He was a perfect gentleman.

'I should have told you to dress casually,' she said,
raising her face for his light kiss. He was wearing a navy
blazer, grey slacks and wing-tips, and his tie was a sober
blue stripe against the white of his shirt. 'It's only a

barbecue, and there will be people there who are barefoot
and wearing jeans.'

He looked surprised. 'If it had been formal, Rebecca,
I'd have worn a suit,' he pointed out.

'What you're wearing isn't exactly casual,' she argued.
'You're not at the bank now, you know.'

'I'm just not comfortable in public dressed for the
beach.'

'But——' She gave up. It would take a while, she
supposed, for Paul to be really relaxed around her family.
After all, she wasn't precisely on hugging terms with his
parents yet, either. And as far as clothes were concerned,
Paul was probably right, After all, his daily attire was
grey pinstripes and dark blue suits with waistcoats. Of
course he wouldn't feel comfortable in cut-off jeans.

'Well, Dad wouldn't kick you out, no matter what you
were wearing,' she said finally.

Paul smiled. 'I'm sure he'll be very pleased at our
news.'

And he would be, Rebecca told herself. Her father
liked Paul. He was from a solid background; the
Fredericks family had been established in Fultonsville
almost as long as the Barclays had. The Mayor and Paul's
father, who was the president of Fultonsville's only local
bank, had often worked together on some new scheme
for the town's improvement. Yes, Ted Barclay would be
pleased at the announcement of their engagement.

So, she asked herself, why would she have preferred it
if Paul hadn't sounded quite so sure of himself?

The barbecue sounded something like the monkey-house
at the zoo. Screams of delight came from the small
garden pool, where Rebecca's niece and nephew were
entertaining the younger set. On the patio, Ted Barclay
was flipping hamburgers with practised skill over a
charcoal fire. New arrivals came around the house every
few minutes, setting covered dishes and casseroles on the

picnic table, then getting themselves a drink from the impromptu bar and wandering from group to group before straggling back to help themselves to the food. Rebecca looked across the lawn to where Paul was standing, in the long shadow of an oak tree, talking to Brett Hilliard. What, she wondered, were they saying to each other?

She hadn't expected Brett Hilliard to be present. The show had been set up for morning taping, she had been told, because he had to be back in Chicago and couldn't be on the programme live. But here he was, large as life, looking as if he had just got off his yacht. As she watched, he pushed a battered white hat back from his eyes.

'He must pack for all occasions,' she muttered.

Beside Rebecca, her sister glanced across the lawn and closed her eyes again. 'You seem to have Hilliard on the brain,' she observed.

'What? Did I say something?'

Gwen Wallace sat up. 'I merely observed that for a woman engaged less than twenty-four hours ago to one man, you are paying an awful lot of attention to another one.'

'It's my job, Gwen.'

'Well, you aren't working at the moment. Would you lay off Brett? He's a perfectly nice guy.'

'Oh?' Rebecca tipped the lemon slice into her glass of tea and stirred it. 'And how would you know? You've been home less than a week.'

'I knew him in college.'

'At Bradley?' Rebecca studied her sister thoughtfully. 'How well did you know him?'

'He was in business school there.' Gwen sounded just a little shy, as if she regretted bringing it up at all. 'We worked on some of the drama department productions together. I dated him sometimes.'

'Oh, really? I thought you were going steady with Bill then. He was your high-school sweetheart——'

Gwen coloured a little. 'Oh, come on, Rebecca. Bill was three hundred miles away. I had to have something to do at weekends, and Brett was—well, Bill didn't mind, anyway. Brett was safe.'

Rebecca's eyes narrowed as she stared across the lawn. *Safe* was an adjective she would never have dreamed of applying to Brett Hilliard. 'It must have been a surprise when he turned up here,' she mused.

'Not really. Dad had told me about the negotiations.' She saw Rebecca's raised eyebrows and added defensively, 'Well, there's been nothing secret about it!'

'No,' Rebecca said slowly.

'Oh, confound your idealism, Becky. You're always seeing shady motives where none exist!'

Am I, Rebecca asked herself, or is there something more here? Just why had Gwen come home this summer, leaving her husband behind, and giving no reason except that she needed a break? In seven years of marriage, she had never done it before ...

Stop it, Rebecca, she ordered herself. Surely the woman can take a vacation without having secret motives!

'So what did Dad say?' Gwen asked. 'Did he approve of your announcement?'

Gwen had made it obvious, Rebecca thought, that the subject of Brett Hilliard was closed. She shrugged. 'I'm twenty-four. It isn't up to him to approve. But yes, he seemed happy about it.' Ted Barclay had looked her over carefully when she had shown him the ring, and then he had given her a bear-hug. What else could she expect, after all, Rebecca asked herself. It was only her imagination that said there had been reserve behind her father's response.

'When's the wedding to be, anyway?'

'We haven't decided. Christmas time, I suppose.'

'That would be nice. Red roses and holly and mistletoe—how appropriate. You'll be booking the whole country club for the reception, I suppose.'

Rebecca said, 'I think we'll have a small wedding.'

'It could be just as elegant,' Gwen agreed. 'But I doubt that you'll have any luck in keeping the guest-list under control. Between Dad's political cronies and the Fredericks' customers at the bank——'

'I hadn't even thought about that.'

'A lot of people will be hurt if they're left out.'

'Well, they'll just have to understand that it's my wedding, not Dad's, and not take offence.'

Gwen didn't answer. 'I'll be happy to help out all I can, while I'm here. I'll start by reminding Dad that a daughter's wedding is not a suitable occasion for a campaign rally. I make no promises about Cleo Fredericks, though.'

'She shouldn't be any problem,' Rebecca said. 'The wedding is the bride's responsibility, anyway. All Mrs Fredericks has to do is supply her guest-list——' She broke off. 'I see what you mean.'

Gwen was looking at her in disbelief. 'She's going to be your mother-in-law and you're still calling her Mrs Fredericks?'

'Well—she's never invited me to do otherwise. What am I supposed to do, go put my arms around her and say, "Hi, Mom"?'

'I should hope not. The thought of Cleo Fredericks taking our mother's place gives me the hives. But——'

'There hasn't been a chance, Gwen. I'm having lunch with her tomorrow. I'm, sure we'll get everything ironed out——'

A cheerful voice from across the patio called, 'Rebecca! Gwen! You're the last, and if you want to eat, you'd better do it now. In ten minutes I'm going to stop cooking and go and watch Brett on *Talk of the Town*!'

'Oh, lord!' Rebecca groaned. 'Only Dad would make it part of the evening's entertainment.'

'Why shouldn't he? I thought you'd enjoy it, Rebecca.

You get to be the star and see the show, too. Sounds like the best of all possible worlds to me.'

The food table had been plundered. They garnished their hamburgers, dug the last of the potato salad out of the bowl, and sat down at the picnic table. A crowd was already gathering on the patio, around the colour television set that Ted Barclay had rolled out from the family-room. One of them called across the lawn. 'Hey, Brett! Come and watch yourself on television!'

'Why bother?' the answer came back. 'I was there!'

'That's some relief,' Rebecca muttered. Despite her best intentions, she couldn't keep her eyes off the set.

There was dead silence on the patio throughout the entire show. Even during the commercials, no one spoke. Once, Gwen turned to look at Rebecca with an odd, questioning expression, but she didn't say anything. Rebecca sat quietly, her hamburger forgotten on the plate, and watched herself make the attempt to cut Brett Hilliard into ribbons. It wasn't a very flattering picture of her, she decided.

Even more irritating was the fact that Jack Barnes had not edited the last remark, when Brett Hilliard had invited her to dinner to discuss the matter. She came out looking like a real fool, she thought morosely.

When the end credits started to roll, the group on the patio turned to stare at her. 'My God, Rebecca——' one of them said. Paul was looking at her with horror. Two furrows cut deeply between Gwen's eyes as she studied her sister.

Ted Barclay's deep voice cut through the murmurs. 'Rebecca,' he said sadly, 'I had no idea, when you talked to me about this project, that you felt so strongly,' he said. 'You always ate so much chocolate when you were a child that I thought you'd be delighted to have a plant right here where it was handy——'

'Stop trying to turn it into a joke, Dad,' she said. 'You know it's got nothing to do with chocolate. It wouldn't matter to me what he was producing——'

'I can see that,' one of the members of the City Council said. 'Why are you so determined to destroy Brett Hilliard?'

'I'm not!' Rebecca denied hotly. 'It's nothing personal.'

'Well, that's a relief,' said a husky voice over her shoulder.

She shivered a little. So Brett Hilliard had come to watch the show anyway, had he? Or had he only arrived for the aftermath, to see what sort of reaction she got from this crowd. Well, she didn't care. She didn't mind defending her feelings to his face. 'It's just that I've seen this sort of project before. All of you have, and right here in Fultonsville. It's easy to make promises, and hard to keep them. Why should we trust his word? What guarantees do we have that he has Fultonsville's best interests at heart? I'm not exactly against the project——'

'You certainly do a good imitation of it,' said Brett Hilliard smoothly.

She jumped up, anxious to get away from him. 'I think you're all like a bunch of sheep being led to the slaughter, without even asking where you're going!'

'Rebecca,' her father warned. 'You're wording this a bit strongly.'

'Look, Dad, I don't like being the one who's throwing cold water on the idea, but somebody has to ask the unpopular questions. Has anyone here stopped to figure out what's going to happen to property taxes if Mr Hilliard welshes on his agreement? I can multiply—I figure it will cost every homeowner in this town an additional five hundred dollars a year just to pay the interest on the money we're going to borrow to build that plant. Doesn't that bother anyone at all?'

There were a few murmurs and a couple of raised eyebrows. Rebecca was encouraged; at least they had heard her.

'If I make one person here think hard enough to start asking tough questions, I'll have accomplished my purpose,' she said stiffly. 'Now, if you will excuse me, I'm sure you'd rather carry on the discussion without my presence.' She went into the house, and didn't stop until she reached the quiet warmth of the long, narrow conservatory that hugged one wall of the formal living-room. She sank into a porch swing and put her hands to her hot cheeks.

'Typical,' she said. 'The first impulse of the crowd, when they get news they don't like, is to kill the messenger.'

Well, she had done what she could. And she would keep on doing it, too, she decided, no matter who was displeased. She would keep asking those tough questions, and challenging those easy promises, until she accomplished her purpose or went down to glorious defeat. And even if the worst happened, if the City Council agreed to the plan, built the building, spent the money, and then Hilliard Confectioners moved on and left the bills behind——'At least they can't say they weren't warned,' she said aloud.

'You can't blame them for not liking the warning.' In the quiet of the greenhouse, the deep voice, soft as it was, filled the space and seemed to make the glass panels vibrate. 'You did choose an abrasively public way of making your point.'

'As long as I made it, that's all that matters, Mr Hilliard.'

'Oh, I think you've stirred up plenty for them to talk about. Perhaps even enough that they'll dither around for months and make no decision at all, and then Hilliard Confectioners will move somewhere else, and Rebel Barclay can write on today's page of the calendar, "The day I kept Fultonsville from progressing".'

'If you came in here to throw nasty barbs, you can consider your job done.'

'No. I thought you might like to try the product you're making all the fuss about.' He held out a gold foil box. 'It's my contribution to the barbecue, Rebel—please don't take it as a bribe.'

'I prefer to be called Rebecca. It is my name—the station manager came up with the Rebel nonsense when I started working for him.'

'He did a very good job of naming you,' he said solemnly. 'But I'll try to remember your preference. I prefer being called Brett, by the way. Even by my enemies.'

'I'm not your enemy, exactly.' She absently opened the box. 'This is full.'

'I certainly hope so. That's the way it left the factory.' He set the box on the table and sat down beside her in the swing.

'I meant, surely you didn't bring this to me first——' She looked up at him thoughtfully. 'All right, which one's got the cyanide in it?'

'You did say caramels were your favourite,' he said smoothly. 'Actually, I put two more boxes out on the picnic table, but the way the vultures were hovering, I didn't think there would be any left for you by the time you got tired of sulking.'

'I am not sulking.' It was indistinct; she was holding a square candy on her tongue, letting the chocolate coating melt off the caramel centre.

He didn't argue the point. 'Can you get me a copy of the tape of that show, by the way?'

'Why?' she asked suspiciously.

'For my scrapbook.'

'You want to study my method of attack, don't you?'

'Of course not. I just want to watch it now and then to remind myself not to get over-confident. Enemies can pop up anywhere, it seems.'

'That's the second time you've said that. I'm not your

enemy, really. I'd like to see your plant be a part of Fultonsville——'

He hit the side of his head lightly with the heel of his hand. 'Can you recommend a good doctor?' he asked. 'I think my hearing has suddenly malfunctioned.'

'But only if you're going to be a good citizen here.'

'What evidence would you like to see? I could show you my Eagle Scout card, if you like. You see, Rebecca, it came as a bit of a shock to me—being raked over the coals on the air by a girl who's scarcely old enough to talk——'

'I am not a girl,' she said hotly. 'I am a woman, and I'd appreciate being treated as one!'

'Really? In that case——' His arm closed around her with sudden force, and drew her tightly against his chest. His mouth was warm, mobile, gentle against hers, and a tiny flicker of pleasure coursed through her. Then, before she could even protest, the caress was over, she was back on her own side of the porch swing, and he was saying good-naturedly, 'Sorry. I can't think what came over me.'

She eyed him suspiciously, aware that any protest she made now, when he had already apologised, would make her look even more foolish. But she didn't believe a word of it. He had known exactly what he was doing, she thought, and it had been part of a calculated programme to keep her off balance.

She poked through the box of chocolates and found a foil-wrapped square. 'Fortunate for you that my fiancé wasn't around,' she said. 'He wouldn't appreciate that. And just in case you lose your head again, I have a terrific scream, and I won't hesitate to use it.'

'I'll be very careful,' he promised. 'Your fiancé? Do you mean the pretend banker?'

'What on earth makes you refer to Paul that way?'

'Because when I've been in to talk to the senior Mr Fredericks, this one is always following along behind and saying "Yes, sir". It left me with the feeling that he was a little kid dressing up in Daddy's clothes and playing banker.'

'I don't think that's a very nice thing to say.'

'Implying that I was taking the entire town of Fultonsville for a ride wasn't polite either, but it didn't stop you from saying it.'

She sighed. It was true, from his point of view. And yet, if she could only make him understand! 'I've seen this happen before, you know. Have they shown you the shopping-mall out on the edge of town? The promoters said that if the city issued the general obligation bonds, they'd pay all the costs. Of course, when the promoters filed for bankruptcy, the bonds didn't disappear—and the city is still paying off the loan.'

'What's that got to do with me, Rebecca?'

'Because you're making the same deal. If you walk out, the town is stuck.'

'If that doesn't bother the City Council, Rebecca, why are you tying yourself into knots about it?'

'Because the City Council doesn't always listen to what the people want. They hold public hearings and then they do as they think best. Sometimes it's right, sometimes it isn't.'

'And you do have the pulse of the public?'

'I think so. I hear it every day for two hours when people call me to talk about their concerns. Those people would be lucky to get two minutes at a council meeting, but that doesn't make their concerns any less important.'

'And you feel the townspeople are against this?'

'They're scared. It's they who will be paying the property taxes if it turns into another shopping-mall flop.'

'Don't worry.'

'You can't possibly give assurances that it won't flop, Brett.'

'No. But I can assure you I won't sell the council a bill of goods on a shopping-mall. I wouldn't know the first thing about it, you see.'

'Is that supposed to be reassuring?' She put her head back against the lime-green cushion on the swing.

'Yes. Because I do know chocolates, and that's what I plan to do for the rest of my life.'

'In Fultonsville.' There was cynicism in her tone.

'Wherever we decide to locate the plant. I think you've underestimated our investment, Rebecca. The city will put up a single building, but that's only the beginning. Over the next few years, we'll be building an entire complex. The equipment alone will represent an investment of millions. Just the moving costs for getting our present employees down here will be extensive.'

'The equipment can be moved, if you decide to get out of Fultonsville. And I won't believe the plans for additional buildings until I see dirt being bulldozed.'

'I'll invite you to the ground-breaking.'

'You do that. I'll be there, and I'll make a handsome apology to you on the air.'

'I'm looking forward to it.' There was a brief silence. The squeak of the swing had rocked Rebecca almost to sleep by the time he spoke again. 'This is crazy, I suppose, but——'

'What's crazy?' she asked.

'To trust you, when you've already sliced me to ribbons once on the air. But would you be interested in an exclusive? The price is, you have to promise to keep it off the air till the paperwork is signed.'

'*If* the paperwork is signed,' she corrected.

'Yes, if you insist.'

'What's the exclusive?'

'Promise first.'

She shook her head. 'Not till I know the general subject, at least.'

'All right. Tomorrow I'm going to show your father what we plan to do with the site. If you'll give me your word of honour to keep it to yourself, you can come and take the tour with us.'

'Why?' she asked suspiciously.

'Because I think when you see it, you'll have a change of heart.'

'And you'll let me in on all the secret plans?'

'Possibly not *all* of them,' he qualified.

She thought about it. 'No,' she said. 'I don't believe in accepting off-the-record confidences. You could end up giving me no new information at all, and claiming that I couldn't use a thing. It would be a very effective way to shut me up on the subject.'

'Miss Barclay, you have a devious mind.'

'That's the only way I've survived four years in this business.'

'Give it some thought,' he recommended. 'And just in case you're planning a way to sneak around and get the information——'

'I wouldn't stoop to that.'

'You would, and we both know it. We also both know that plot of land is so large and so bare that you couldn't possibly get close enough to us to overhear anything. You could lurk around all morning watching us walk the site and get nothing more than poison ivy for your effort.'

'I'm a reporter, Mr Hilliard, not a sleuth. I do not crawl around building-sites, or listen at corners, or eavesdrop in restaurants——'

'Just remember that you had the chance. It's not my fault if you'd prefer to keep a closed mind. Take the chocolates home with you if you like.'

He moved easily for such a big man; he was gone before she could think of an appropriate retort.

She would have liked to throw the box of chocolates at him. The idea of trying to bribe her with information, to win her over to his side and effectively stop her from saying anything more at all on the question of Hilliard Confectioners! The man was a public relations genius!

Well, his scheme hadn't worked on Rebecca Barclay.

She would continue her investigation, and her attack, and her defence of the taxpayers of Fultonsville, no matter what Brett Hilliard said, thought, or did. And that was that.

Paul was furious. She had never seen him quite so angry before, and it made her sad, as well as irritable. 'This is the best chance Fultonsville has,' he sputtered as he drove her home. 'It may be the last opportunity for this city to make it. If we don't seize this opening, that's the end. Do you want to see Fultonsville become the biggest ghost town on the Mississippi?'

'Of course not. But I don't want to see it bankrupt, either.'

'Do you know what kind of payroll Hilliard puts out every week? Do you have any idea what size line of credit he needs?'

'Oh, I see. The real question you're asking, Paul, is—do I know how much money Fultonsville Bank and Trust will make from this deal? Well, no, I don't, but I have a question in return—have you thought about how much money you will lose if this deal goes sour?'

'Rebecca,' he said stiffly, 'I never before realised what a pessimist you were.'

'Now that's humorous. When I bought my car last year, Paul, you wouldn't lend me the money till I'd filled out ten pounds of paperwork. Now Mr Charming Hilliard sails into town and you're willing to hand him the keys to the vault.'

'It doesn't have keys, Rebecca. It's a time-lock.'

'I do know that, Paul, thank you very much! The point is, everybody trusts the man and no one is asking questions!'

Paul pulled the car up to the gate in front of Rebecca's house. 'Of course we've asked questions,' he said stiffly. 'He has an excellent credit-rating, a recommendation from his present banker——'

'Have you ever considered that the present banker might just be delighted to get rid of him?' She held up a hand. 'You're right; I don't have the slightest bit of evidence to back up that accusation. I just wondered if the possibility had occurred to you.'

He didn't answer. 'I'll see you tomorrow evening,' he said. 'Mother is expecting you at the club tomorrow for lunch, of course, at twelve.'

'That gives me an hour and a half before the show starts. That will be fine. Want to come up for coffee or something?'

He considered. 'It's late, Rebecca.'

'All right. I'll see you tomorrow then.'

She walked up the porch steps, unlocked the big bevelled glass main door, and waved goodbye to him.

I knew that of course we'd have a fight some time, she told herself. But I expected that our first argument would be over money, or wedding plans, or where to spend the honeymoon. I never would have dreamed our first quarrel would be over Brett Hilliard and his stupid chocolate factory!

And Paul didn't even know about the kiss Brett had snatched in the greenhouse tonight. She had meant to tell him, to laugh it off—just in case it ever came up. She had forgotten.

Just as well, she thought. There was no sense in looking for more trouble. Brett Hilliard was capable of causing enough, all by himself.

CHAPTER THREE

AFTER a night of thinking about it, however, Rebecca decided that it would be insane to turn down the opportunity to find out more about Brett Hilliard's plans for that sprawling tract of land on the edge of the town. Even if she couldn't ethically use the information on her show, because of the agreement she would have to make with him, it would be helpful as background. With that kind of knowledge, perhaps she could point a casual finger, and hint to others about where the skeletons lay buried.

That was why, after she stopped at the post office on her regular morning routine, she directed her steps towards the Mayor's red brick and stucco house instead of towards the radio station. She had no idea when the tour would start; Brett had said only that they would go this morning. Fortunately, according to the tiny appointment book she always carried, her entire morning was free.

That was a rare occurence. Even when she didn't have to fill in for another staff member on the air, Rebecca seldom had a morning that wasn't cut up with commitments. Either she was looking for ideas for future shows, or she was working on advertisement campaigns to run in the coming weeks, or she was out in the community doing public relations work for the station. But she loved her job, every long minute of it.

Rebecca glanced at her watch. Already the sun was high, and heat burned down over the dusty streets. But it was fairly early. Surely, after the late barbecue the night before, her father would be having his second cup of coffee and reading the Fultonsville *Chronicle* on the patio.

She was right. Ted Barclay looked up warily when she came around the house, and waved a hand at the coffee pot. She poured herself a cup and sat down.

'Well, look who's here,' Gwen said. She pushed aside a section of the newspaper. 'It's the prodigal daughter in the flesh.'

'I came to catch a ride with you this morning, Dad,' Rebecca said as she stirred a little cream into her coffee.

The newspaper dropped briefly, and over the top of it, Ted Barclay said, 'Rebecca, you live three blocks from the station. We live a half-mile out—in the wrong direction.'

'I didn't mean I wanted to go downtown. I meant that you must be meeting Brett Hilliard somewhere for your tour, and he forgot to tell me where.'

There was an ironic twist to his words. 'Why do I doubt that story, Rebecca?'

'He did invite me. Don't you believe your own daughter?'

'Am I talking to my daughter? Or am I talking to the ace reporter of the radio world? Am I going to be quoted on the air?' He sounded hurt.

Rebecca sighed. She hated it when her reporter's judgement collided with a daughter's respect for her father. But it was bound to happen now and then. Usually they could both keep a sense of humour about it, but this time she wasn't so sure.

'Don't mind him,' Gwen recommended. 'He's been like this since he got up. He's just a grouchy old bear this morning.'

'You really are upset about last night, then,' Rebecca said.

'What did you expect, that I'd stand up and applaud, Becky?' he said plaintively, 'I've spent the best part of a year behind the scenes, trying to work out this deal. I am not irresponsible when it comes to the public trust or the taxpayers' money. I have asked all the questions——'

'Then, if you have answers that satisfy you, you shouldn't mind passing them on to those who are less fortunate than you,' Rebecca said briskly. 'There are some of us who haven't heard them from the man himself. So why don't you join your protegé on *Rebel with a Cause* next week and tell the public all about it?'

Ted groaned. 'Why do I feel as if I'm being manipulated?'

'Because you are,' Gwen said. 'Rebecca, I haven't seen you so upset at anybody since that little boy in elementary school used to call you Carrots and pull your hair. I can't think what's causing all the fireworks, but——'

'Fireworks,' Ted said. 'Didn't we have enough fireworks to please you on Independence Day? You have to go dig up your own?'

'I'm only asking——'

'Have you ever considered a summer cruise, Rebecca? I'll pay your way. Or if you want to get out of the heat, I've heard Alaska is very nice this time of year. I'll buy you a one-way ticket to Anchorage——'

'I don't want to get out of the heat, Dad. I enjoy my job, and I like the trust the public puts in me to represent them to the best of my ability.'

'At the moment, your best effort looks pretty feeble. The idea of sneaking in here this morning and expecting that I'd actually believe that Brett invited you to come along——'

'Hello, Brett,' Gwen said sweetly. 'Have a cup of coffee and watch the fight. It's only the third round, but we may have to settle for a technical knockout.'

'No, thanks, Gwen.' He smiled down at her and laid a hand on her shoulder. Gwen patted his fingers. It seemed to be a casual, friendly gesture. Rebecca thought, I wonder how much she's seeing of him . . . 'I'm anxious to get out to the plant site before the temperature goes any higher,' Brett went on. 'I see you changed your mind about coming with us, Rebecca.'

Ted Barclay choked on his coffee.

Rebecca made a face at her father. 'Yes, I have. Exclusive rights to the story, I believe you said, in return for my not announcing your building plans until you give the go-ahead.'

'Close enough.'

'Do you want that in writing?'

He looked her over, impassively. 'No.'

'I'm glad you trust my word.'

'I don't. But I've thought of some ways in which I can assure you'll keep your promise. Shall we go?'

Rebecca picked up her handbag, shoving her mail deeper into one of the side pockets, and swung it over her shoulder. He was joking, she thought. He just couldn't stand to let her get the better of him.

'I hope you're wearing your walking-shoes,' he said.

He looked quite prepared for a hike himself today, she thought. He was wearing faded jeans and running-shoes and a pullover shirt that made his eyes look green and which did nothing to conceal his powerful shoulders. I wonder if he backpacks, she thought.

'Have a good time,' Gwen said as they left the patio. 'In this heat, I'm glad it's you instead of me.'

Brett opened the rear door of his car with a flourish. A Cadillac, Rebecca noted, with interest. An almost-new Cadillac, the colour of highly polished copper.

'Sorry about the mess in the car,' he said. 'As soon as the tour is finished, I'm off to Chicago, so I checked out of the hotel this morning to save time. You did tell me last night that you weren't coming,' he reminded Rebecca as he shifted a briefcase and a duffel bag to the floor on the other side of the car.

'It won't bother me in the least,' she assured him politely. She climbed in, tossed her handbag on top of the pile, and relaxed against the cream-coloured leather upholstery.

Ted Barclay didn't regain his voice till they were nearly out of town. Finally, he said, jerking a thumb over his shoulder at Rebecca. 'Why did you bring her? If these plans are top-secret——'

'I thought it was safer to have her where I could watch her,' Brett replied. 'Hard to tell what she would have been plotting if we'd left her in town.'

She could see his reflection in the driving-mirror, so she stuck her tongue out at him. He grinned, suddenly, and laugh wrinkles gathered around his eyes. He should do that more often, she thought. It's quite attractive.

And you, my girl, are here on business, and not to admire the scenery, she reminded herself. She slid up on to the edge of the seat and pointed ahead at a mammoth cream-coloured brick building surrounded by asphalt parking. 'That's the shopping mall I was telling you about last night, Brett,' she said.

'Oh, yes,' Ted Barclay said. 'Plenty of room there for expansion. The retail district will be able to grow very quickly——'

'What that means,' Rebecca interrupted, 'is that it's more than half empty at the moment, because no major retailers want to put a store in a depressed area like this. The city loses money on the rents every month.'

'Rebecca,' the mayor said wearily, 'remind me to tell the Chamber of Commerce that if you ever apply for a job, they should close up shop and leave town. You're not supposed to be discouraging the man, for heaven's sake——'

'I'm telling the truth. If that discourages him, then better we should find out now, before he's started to spend the city's money.'

The Cadillac swung into the industrial park, where a few scattered buildings housed the small manufacturing plants that had survived the town's decline. 'That one used to be a car-parts plant,' Rebecca said, pointing to a huge steel building. 'It had three hundred workers. Then the company closed down, and sold the building, and now they make shipping crates in one wing of it and employ fifty people.'

'I know,' Brett said. 'They're going to bid on our box contracts. It will be awfully convenient, if they can come up with a competitive price. Besides that, it means that somewhere in this town are a couple of hundred people who have experience on an assembly line. Did you ever think of that, Miss Civic Improvement?' He pulled the car up at the edge of a flat acreage, where tiny orange surveyors' flags fluttered in the breeze, marking the boundaries.

'I wouldn't bet that those people are still here,' she muttered.

Ted ignored her. 'Have you ever thought of starting a retail outlet?' he asked Brett. 'There's a nice little corner shop in the mall, reasonable rent, good location——'

'His Honour thinks it would be a tourist attraction.' Rebecca seemed to be addressing a puffy cloud as she got out of the Cadillac. 'As a matter of fact,' she added thoughtfully, 'it probably would be.'

Within ten minutes she was wishing that she had worn jeans; she was hot and sweaty from scrambling across the weedy ground after the two men. She was grateful that at least she was wearing sensible shoes; in anything with a heel, she would surely have broken an ankle by now.

She caught up with them just as Brett said, 'The air-conditioning system is the most important thing, of course.'

'I can imagine it in the summer,' she said dreamily. 'The system breaks down, and there are rivers of chocolate flowing out of every door . . . Milk chocolate, dark chocolate——'

'Nightmarish, isn't it?' said Brett.

The Mayor shook his head. 'Not to Rebecca. This is

the nearest thing to a genuine chocolate addict that there is. She'd be out here with a spoon, trying to clean up the mess single-handed.'

'Actually,' said Brett, 'I have an idea about that for the future. The plant gets hot, of course, because of the furnaces, and the air-conditioning in the storage areas has a hard time. But—come here and I'll show you.'

'How far back does this land go?' Rebecca panted as she stumbled across the gravelly surface, trying to keep up with his long strides. 'I thought it was only the flat section.'

'That's all that anybody's used,' the Mayor said, making a sweeping gesture that took in the plain formed by generations of silt deposited by the mighty river, before its course had changed slightly and left the perfect location for a town. 'But it goes up into the hills.'

'And that's exactly what I want to use,' said Brett. 'We can burrow back into these hills and put in a storage terminal for the finished chocolates. A few feet down, we'll hit a constant temperature that's just right for long-term storage. The trucks or wagons can load from this end, right on the side of the hill, and we won't have to count on man-made cooling.'

'Ingenious,' said Ted Barclay.

'Also secret,' Brett added, with a meaningful glance at Rebecca.

They wandered over the site for another hour, with Brett pointing out features of the land that would be helpful to the new plant. They paced out the approximate dimensions of the building, the car park, and the loading docks. They talked about putting in a railhead, so that supplies could be transferred from the river barges to the plant by a special narrow-gauge train.

And by the time they walked back to the car, dusty and hot, Rebecca understood why her father was so confident of this young man. She still didn't entirely believe him, but he wasn't only charming, he made sense. And yet, when she looked critically at the whole thing, she kept coming back to the beginning—the fact that there were no guarantees. The whole thing depended on one man's word.

'You are certain this is going to go through, aren't you?' she challenged Brett as they drove back to town.

'No.'

'But you've got architects' drawings, and surveyors' reports, and——'

'Would you like to see the ones on the other two cities we're seriously considering?'

'Rebecca, Fultonsville is not the only town interested,' Ted Barclay pointed out. 'If there was anything wrong with this deal, do you think half a dozen towns would all be manoeuvring to get this plant?'

'That's one of my big concerns,' she said. 'That those towns will still be sweetening the deal in a couple of years.'

Ted shrugged, as if he was giving up. 'Would you mind dropping me at City Hall?' he asked. 'I hate to ask you to be a taxi service, Brett, but I have a noon meeting, and I'm already late.'

Noon? Rebecca stared at her watch, unbelieving. It was ten minutes past twelve. 'Oh, no,' she said. 'Cleo Fredericks is waiting for me at the country club. Would you drop me off, Brett?'

For an instant, he looked as if he was considering reasons to say no. Then he nodded and stopped the car in the traffic lane directly in front of City Hall. Rebecca slid out to take Ted Barclay's place in the front seat.

'When you talk about this morning, Rebecca,' the Mayor recommended, 'use your head.'

An impatient driver behind them honked his horn, and Rebecca hurried back into the car.

'Cleo?' Brett said thoughtfully as he threaded through the traffic. 'Is she related to the pretend banker?'

'She's his mother.'

'And you're keeping your future mother-in-law waiting? Naughty, naughty.'

'I forgot to watch the time. Not that it would have done any good; if you'd known I had an appointment, you'd have made certain I was late.'

'Now why would I have done that?' Brett asked thoughtfully. 'It's to my advantage for you to be busy with the banker. It keeps your mind off other things. See you Wednesday afternoon for Round Two.'

Rebecca was out of breath when she arrived at the door of the country club's dining-room. Would Cleo even have waited for her, she wondered, in the instant before she saw the woman across the room. Cleo Fredericks, Rebecca thought, would always be the perfect lady in public. She was wearing a pastel floral print and a wide-brimmed white hat with a pastel scarf forming a sort of trailing veil. She looked cool and charming and as if she had just stepped from the pages of an etiquette book. Rebecca half-expected her to be wearing white gloves.

But it didn't take intuition to know that underneath the public façade, Cleo was coldly furious. She glanced at her delicate diamond-studded wristwatch as Rebecca hurried towards the table, and said, with a frigid smile, 'I'm so sorry we couldn't find a more convenient time for you, Rebecca. If you'd only let me know this was an inopportune day——'

'Oh, it isn't!' Rebecca said breathlessly. 'I was just very busy this morning, and the time slipped away——' I'm only getting myself in deeper, she thought. She was unpleasantly aware of the fact that her hair needed combing and her clothes were dusty. She had taken a quick glance at her reflection in the glass door as she came in, and had decided not to delay any longer by stopping in the ladies' room to freshen up. Apparently, the decision had been a mistake. She suspected, from the way Cleo was looking at her, that there was a streak of dirt right across her nose.

Should she excuse herself for a moment and go and wash her face? No, she told herself firmly. She'd stick with the natural look, and if Cleo couldn't understand that her job sometimes required her to get into some unladylike situations, that was Cleo's problem and not Rebecca's.

She told the waitress firmly that she would like a cup of coffee. She was scheduled to go on the air, and even if she hadn't been, she wouldn't want to give Cleo Fredericks the idea that she was in the habit of drinking alcohol at lunch. She thought regretfully about a tall glass of wine cooler. At the moment it would have tasted wonderful. Or a Bloody Mary, salty and biting . . .

Not in front of your mother-in-law, she told herself. There is no sense in letting her think you're a souse as well as unpunctual and careless about your appearance.

'I thought we should start discussing the wedding plans,' Cleo said. 'Paul said you'd decided on a date in early December.'

That's news to me, Rebecca thought. 'We hadn't set a day, actually. We'd talked about a winter wedding, but——'

'Since this is August, it will be very important to start planning immediately,' Cleo went on. 'When Paul's sister was married, we had a full year, and we needed every day of it. Why, just to have her dress designed and made took five months.' She calculated, and said, 'I suppose you'll have to settle for a ready-made one. There simply isn't time for a designer gown.'

Rebecca was tempted to retort that she had seen a very nice wedding dress in her size at a rummage sale just yesterday. But she swallowed the incendiary comment and said, 'I'm afraid so, Mrs Fredericks.'

'Of course, as soon as you've set a date we'll have to see about reserving the country club. I'm certain your father will want to have plenty of room for the reception. We have many friends in common, of course, but I'm sure that we will need the entire clubhouse. You'll be having a catered dinner, of course.'

Rebecca noted with interest that it was not a question. 'Well, we really hadn't——'

'It's going to be difficult for you, I'm sure, to make your father understand that he simply cannot put these things off. It's so unfortunate that your dear mother died; she would have understood. Men seem to think that a wedding can be planned in a matter of days. Really, Rebecca, you're going to have to set a date no later than next week. Heaven knows it's important to get your photographer lined up right away, and the caterer. The band for the dance is just as criticial. The flowers can wait a little while, I suppose——'

Rebecca's chicken salad arrived. She began to pick at it. There was no problem with minding her table manners, she noted; it was impossible to talk with one's mouth full when one didn't get a chance to say a single word!

'You'll have to begin asking your attendants right away, too. Christmas time—it might be a little difficult for them to arrange to travel. Paul's cousin has a little girl who I'm sure would be delighted to be your flower girl——'

'I have a niece,' Rebecca broke in. 'If I decide I want a flower girl, which I'm not at all certain of.'

'I don't mean anything against your niece, Rebecca, but Paul's cousin's daughter has been flower girl in at least six weddings.

'Then perhaps she would enjoy watching mine from a seat in the church,' Rebecca said sweetly.

Cleo raised an arched eyebrow. 'I can think of at least three of Paul's cousins who would be terribly hurt if they weren't asked to be bridesmaids. I'm sure you'll have a few choices of your own, too. That means half a dozen at least. We'll simply have to have a full-time dressmaker to get it all done in time.'

I am not going to argue with her, Rebecca told herself firmly. It is Paul's business to tell her that it is our wedding, and that it is not up to her to arrange it. I'll tell him tonight that he simply must stop her from carrying on this way.

She listened patiently while Cleo told her all about Paul's sister's wedding, down to the colours of the ribbons that tied the flowers that decorated the candle-holders on the end of each pew. And it was with deep relief that she finally excused herself and walked from the club to the radio station. If she had been lunching with anyone but Cleo, she would have begged a ride, for the afternoon sun was blistering on the asphalt pavements. But she was afraid that Cleo would use the time to tell her what pattern of crystal goblets Paul's sister's guests had used to toast the bride and groom.

She was on time to the minute, but she didn't even have time to stop in her office and brush her hair. 'Fortunately, it's only radio,' she muttered. She had settled herself in the broadcast-booth, ready to take over from the young disc jockey in the control-room at the stroke of two o'clock, when Jack Barnes came in.

'I heard you weren't content with the show,' he said. 'You had to rip up at Brett Hilliard at the party last night too.'

'What's eating you, Jack?'

'The station manager isn't very happy, that's what's eating me. You know he's in favour of this thing.'

'All he's interested in is advertising revenues.'

'That's where your pay comes from.'

'Jack, we both know that my contract states he doesn't have editorial control of what I say on the air, much less at a private party. You can remind him of that for me, if you like.'

'Do you have to make such a big deal of it, Rebel? Nobody else is getting upset about Hilliard.'

'If you think about it, Jack, you'll know that's exactly

why I am making a big deal of it.'

In the control-room, the disc jockey was waving frantically. Rebecca plugged in the cartridge that held the theme music of her show and flicked the switch that let her special phone number bypass the regular switchboard. The phone lines were already lighting up when the theme ended.

This was her favourite part of the job, she thought, sitting here talking to ordinary people about ordinary problems. The very unexpectedness and unpredictability was the thing she liked best; she never knew when she answered a call whether it would be a battered wife wanting help, a citizen upset at government, or a housewife wanting to track down a favourite recipe. Rebel loved every minute of it.

'Good afternoon, everybody. On a beautiful day like this, with the sun pouring down, what are you doing inside listening to the radio, anyway?' That statement ought to give Jack Barnes apoplexy, she thought. 'I know, you're inside *because* it's so blasted hot, aren't you? Now that's sensible of you! I'm Rebel, and thank you for joining me on *Rebel with a Cause*. We don't have a guest today, so the show will be an open forum. What's on your minds? Do you want to talk about the Hilliard Confectioners deal? Would you rather swap a few tall tales? Some people in town would say those are actually the same thing.'

Jack Barnes rolled his eyes and left the broadcasting booth, closing the door carefully because the microphone was live. Rebecca was reasonably sure he'd have liked to slam it. She smiled and punched in the first telephone call.

'Hello, Rebel, honey,' said a quavery old voice.

'Good afternoon, Mrs Henderson.' The old woman was a favourite, a regular caller. Rebecca thought she was simply lonely, and calling the radio station gave her something to do with her afternoons. She was seldom concerned about public causes unless the garbage company was threatening to raise rates.

'I saw you last night on the television,' Mrs Henderson went on. 'You looked mighty pretty talking to that handsome young man. Is he married or single?'

Rebel swallowed a smile. 'Well, I don't know, Mrs Henderson.'

'And just why don't you know?'

'I forgot to ask him.'

Mrs Henderson sighed, as if faced with a particularly difficult pupil. 'Rebel, honey, now just when are you going to stop arguing with young men like that and start looking at them as possible husbands? It's no way to make a good impression on a man by sitting there quarrelling with him.'

Rebel thought that Jack Barnes, if he was listening to the show in his office, was probably applauding. There was no point in trying to explain to Mrs Henderson that her job did not involve making a good impression on her guests.

'You're not getting any younger, you know,' Mrs Henderson finished.

Rebecca made a mental note to amend the job description in her personnel file as soon as the show was over. *Needs fantastic sense of humour*, she would add.

'Mrs Henderson, I'm surprised you didn't notice my left hand last night on the show. I'm wearing a new ring.'

'A wedding ring?' the old woman screeched.

'No. But the next best thing.' Now that it was too late to back out of an announcement, Rebecca was suffering pangs of doubt. Not that it was any secret, of course, and as long as Paul's parents and her own father had been told, there was no point in delaying. Too late, she told herself, and went on, 'I'm engaged to marry Paul Fredericks. He's a vice-president of Fultonsville Bank and Trust, you know.'

'A banker.' Mrs Henderson's voice oozed pride. 'Well,

now, that puts a different look on things. A hometown boy, at that. I'm real proud of you, Rebel.'

'Thank you, Mrs Henderson. I'll let you know all about the plans for the wedding.' With a silent sigh of relief, she eased Mrs Henderson off the telephone and picked up the next call.

For the next two hours she juggled calls, commercials, weather reports, and news spots, and when the show was finished she sat back with a satisfied sigh and reached for her handbag. Her time was her own, now that the artifical limits of the broadcast world had been satisfied, and the first thing she was going to do was brush her hair, as she had been wanting to do since she got out of Brett Hilliard's car at the country club.

Her handbag wasn't under the control console where she always put it. She frowned a little, and remembered that she hadn't stopped in her office at all. That meant that she hadn't had the bag when she came into the station.

'Smart,' she groaned. 'You have to go and leave your handbag in the dining-room at the country club. Nothing like making an idiot of yourself.' She refused to think about what might happen if someone had found it and taken it; every credit card she owned was in that bag, along with her cheque book and her wallet.

When she called the country club, the manager was concerned and apologetic but absolutely unhelpful. No, no bag had been turned in. Yes, he'd be happy to go and look. No, there was nothing under the table Mrs Fredericks had reserved for lunch. No, he was quite sure that no one could have taken the bag. The table hadn't been used again, as the dining-room had closed shortly after Mrs Fredericks had left.

She gave up. 'All right, Rebecca,' she told herself. 'Let's start from the beginning.' She had left her apartment, stopped at the post office, tucked her unopened mail into a side pocket of the bag, walked out to her father's house, sat down for coffee, stuck the bag under her chair——

'I'll bet I left it there,' she muttered, and dialled her father's number. 'Did I leave my handbag on the patio this morning?' she asked, when Gwen answered.

'Nope.'

'That was quick. You're sure?'

'Absolutely. I can see the patio from here—I'm lying beside the pool with the cordless phone.'

'I can tell by the crackle on the line. But are you sure it isn't around there somewhere?'

She could hear Gwen calling to her two children, and the muted splash of water. Then Gwen said, 'Neither of the kids has seen it. And I'm certain you were carrying it when you left. I noticed that you hadn't opened your mail. It only stuck in my mind because I can't stand it till I've torn open every envelope.'

That was definite, Rebecca thought. 'All right. If I had it when I left there . . . I got into Brett's car, and put it on the seat beside me——'

And left it there when she moved to the front seat of the car in front of City hall. 'Damn,' she said.

'Is it permanently lost? I did that once. Cancelling all my credit cards was a nightmare. I really thought Bill was going to murder me.'

'No,' Rebecca said morosely. 'I know exactly where it is.'

'Then there's no problem.'

'It's on the back seat of Brett Hilliard's car, on its way to Chicago,' she said. 'He doesn't even know it's there. And he isn't coming back to town till next Tuesday.'

CHAPTER FOUR

AND Tuesday was five very long days away. After Rebecca had said goodbye to Gwen, she sat for a long time in the broadcast-booth, her aching head propped on her hand. Her cheque book, credit cards, and wallet—all had gone north for a vacation. Not only was she without cash, but she wouldn't even be able to get money out of her bank account. Not that there was much in there, she reflected. She had forgotten to deposit her pay cheque yesterday.

'So I'll just cash it instead,' she said, and then remembered, with a sick sinking feeling, that she had tucked the slip of yellow paper down into the side of her handbag, right next to her car keys, so that she wouldn't forget to take care of it today. 'Idiot!' she told herself finally. 'You don't have any money, you don't have car keys, you can't even get into your apartment——'

And worst of all, she thought, Brett Hilliard didn't even know the bag was there. He would find it when he unloaded his car, of course, but when would that be? And what if in the meantime he left the car parked somewhere, and someone glanced in and realised that a handbag was there for the taking? People broke car windows sometimes to steal things like that, and a handbag left on the back seat of a Cadillac would be the most tempting of targets.

'And if that happens,' she muttered, 'he'll blame me for the damage to his car!'

She would have to find him, that was all there was to it. Perhaps he would send the bag back to her, overnight express.

She walked home, knocked on the door of the

landlord's apartment, and told his wife that she had locked herself out. She let herself into her apartment with the borrowed key and looked morosely out of the window at her car. It was useless, without her keys. At least she had parked it off to the side, where it would be out of the other tenants' way.

When she caught up with her father, and asked if he had Brett's home telephone number, there was an ages-long silence before he said, politely, 'Do you want to do a long-distance interview?'

'No, I want to call him up and do some heavy breathing,' Rebecca snapped. 'I'm sure an obscene phone call would make his day. Would you just give me the number, Dad?'

'I don't have it.'

'What do you mean, you don't——'

'I'll give you his office number.'

Rebecca glanced at her watch. It was probably too late in the day to do anything; the factory was no doubt closed by now. But at least she could try. She dialled the number and thanked her lucky stars that the telephone company let her call anywhere she wanted as long as she paid the bill at the end of the month; if they had insisted on cash in advance, she would have been in real trouble. She sorted through the kitchen catch-all drawer while she listened to the telphone ring and found a nickel, a dime, and seven cents. 'Wow,' she said. 'I can buy half a candy bar.'

The switchboard at Hilliard Confectioners sounded doubtful that anyone would still be in the executive offices at this late hour, but Rebecca's crossed fingers paid off, and a moment later a warm, feminine voice was asking what she could do to help.

With a voice like that, Rebecca thought, I bet she's pretty. She told the secretary the whole story. 'And if I could just have Mr Hilliard's home number,' she finished, 'so I can make arrangements to get my handbag back——'

'I'm very sorry. I'm not authorised to give out that information.' The secretary did sound regretful, but also very firm. 'I will give Mr Hilliard your message——'

'But don't you see? The thing that really worries me is that he doesn't know it's there, and if someone should steal it——'

'I'll give him the message, Miss Barclay.'

Rebecca sighed. There would be no moving that woman; she knew the signs. Brett Hilliard had his secretary well trained.

She put the telephone down and started to search through the cupboards. At least she could eat, she reflected irritably. She didn't keep a large stock of food on hand, but she made it a point never to run out, either. It was just that towards the end of the week, the menu lost a little variety. And this week, she concluded as she rearranged the shelves, it was going to be downright dull; she had been planning to stop at the supermarket on her way home from the radio station tonight, right after she banked her pay cheque . . .

She was reading an old magazine and absently eating macaroni and cheese when the telephone rang. That would be Paul, she thought. He was probably calling to tell her when he would be over. She would have to explain to him tonight why he must straighten his mother out immediately, before Cleo started making arrangements for a fancy wedding . . .

'I understand you're looking for me,' a baritone voice murmured into her ear.

She almost dropped the telephone. 'Brett!'

'You remembered my name. It's a nice change to hear excitement in your voice instead of loathing.'

'I thought it would be morning before you got my message.'

'It probably would have been if I hadn't checked in

with my secretary when I got home.'

'Am I ever glad you did!'

'She wasn't quite sure if it was a real problem, though, or if it was just a gimmick to get my attention.'

'Why, you conceited—it's a real problem, Your Arrogance! I wouldn't be calling you up just to hear the music of your voice, that's sure!'

'Some women do.'

'They have my deepest sympathy.'

'I'm single, if that's what you wanted to know.'

'What?' Rebecca was startled.

'I was listening to your show while I drove, till I got out of range. I thought it might be prudent to know how you conduct yourself on your own show. Actually, I thought you handled the lady's question very well—you didn't even sound curious.'

'I'm not. But I'll be sure to pass the information on to Mrs Henderson.'

'No, you won't. You don't want to admit you've been talking to me outside business hours. What did you want, anyway, if it wasn't to check out my marital status?'

'I left my handbag on the back seat of your car. I hope you keep it locked.'

'In this city? Do you know what the life expectancy of an unlocked Cadillac is in Chicago? Why do you think I want to move?'

She relaxed a little. 'Then you still have it. I called because I can't do without my bag for five days.'

She could almost hear the shrug in his words. 'You must forgive me if I don't understand. I've never lost one myself, you see.'

'A handbag? I should hope not. You have no idea how important it is, Brett. I can't even drive my car——'

'You don't have a spare set of keys?'

'Of course I do. I keep them in the inside pocket of my bag, so that I don't lock myself out.'

'That sounds like you, Rebecca.'

'To say nothing of money and other important things——'

'Would you like me to wire you some money?' He sounded concerned.

Rebecca closed her eyes in pain. She could imagine what would happen if the Western Union office at the corner drugstore got a money order from Brett Hilliard for Rebecca Barclay. The news would be all over town in minutes, and everyone would want to know why. 'No, thanks. It isn't only money, you see——'

'I know. Don't you realise that your birth certificate ought to be locked up somewhere? And hasn't anyone ever told you not to carry your passport around with you, Rebecca? Unless you're planning to make a sudden trip out of the country, of course. Do you know what a legitimate passport is worth to a thief?'

'Have you been rummaging through my handbag?'

'I had to find out who it belonged to,' he pointed out reasonably.

'Who else could have left it there? How many women have been riding around in your car today?' Rebecca howled.

'Why do you ask? Are you jealous? You should be grateful that an honest guy like me is the one who has your bag.'

'I used to be!'

'Now, Rebecca. I'll be back in town on Tuesday——'

'I can't do without my make-up kit and my appointment calendar from now until Tuesday!' She was almost shouting.

'I see. Now we get to the really important things. Mere money—no, you can always borrow some from your boyfriend. If, that is, you have collateral. On the other hand——'

'Will you send me the darn thing, overnight express?'

'Collect, I suppose?'

'Of course not. How would I pay for it? I promise I'll

give you your money back.'

'You know that there's a seven-pound limit on packages, and I don't think this will fit. How do you carry it around all the time? It weighs a ton.'

'My appointment calendar doesn't weigh seven pounds! And you could throw in my pay cheque and my credit cards——'

'Sorry. I think all the courier services are closed by now. Besides, I have a date tonight.'

'You could ask your secretary to do it,' Rebecca snapped. 'Then perhaps she'd believe I'm not trying to vamp you!'

'Nope. She's the one I have the date with.'

She wanted to cry, but she didn't think that tears would move him. 'All right,' she said, determined to keep her temper. 'You've made it obvious that you aren't going to send it back.'

'I've got a better idea. Why don't you take the commuter train in the morning and come up and get it?'

'Using what to buy my ticket?'

'I'll book it and put it on my American Express card. You might find it an interesting weekend, Rebecca.'

Ice tinkled in her voice. 'If you think for one second that I am the kind of girl who would consider spending a weekend rendezvous with you——'

'Now wait a minute. Aren't you jumping to conclusions? Did I say anything about snuggling up together for the weekend? I just said you'd find it interesting.'

'I know your kind. It's obvious what you had in mind.'

'I was thinking about showing you around the present plant, explaining why we want to move, that sort of thing. I thought if you could see it for yourself, you might get off this high horse of yours about how I'm out to pull a con on Fultonsville. But I see you'd rather remain happily ignorant.'

She was silent for a moment. You idiot, Rebecca, she told herself—jumping to the conclusion that he was inviting you to spend an intimate weekend in his city hideaway! 'Sorry,' she said stiffly. 'I'd forgotten about your secretary, or I wouldn't have made such a foolish mistake.'

'Don't be jealous of her. She's only second-best. I'd much rather have you.'

'I'll bet she wouldn't appreciate being called second-best.'

'It's true. You really should believe me, Rebecca. I'm down on my knees at this very moment, pleading with you to take pity on me and end my loneliness——'

'Of course you are,' she agreed. 'Too bad I can't see you and get the full effect. Would you be serious for two minutes and at least read me the entries in my appointment book?'

'I am perfectly serious.' But his sense of humour seemed uninjured. 'Would you like me to read your mail, too? I see you didn't have time to open it.'

'No, thanks. I'll wait till I get it back.'

'There are a couple of things here that are pretty intriguing. One of them is from another candy company, and it says in big red letters that it's your stockholder's proxy forms. Is that why you're so opposed to my building a plant in Fultonsville? Do you own a lot of stock in my competition?'

'None of your business.'

'That's the worst part of proxy statements,' he mused. 'It's obvious what they are, but the envelopes are so thick you can't read through them. I suppose I could go put the kettle on and steam it open, but——'

'My appointment book, please, Brett.'

'Why are you in such a hurry? I'm paying for this call. Or don't you want to talk about my competition?'

'All right, I'll explain it. Dad gave me three shares as a gag gift once. He said I ate so much chocolate I ought to be a stockholder. Now will you read me my appointments?'

'Your show tomorrow is the flower lady, whatever that means.'

'She's going to talk about the messages that flowers hold. You know, roses stand for grace and beauty, daisies mean innocence, jonquils for desire, all that sort of thing.'

'Fascinating. Too bad I'm too far away to listen in. I might learn something.'

'I suspect you already know it all. Anything else?'

'Public relations appearance in the morning, at—I can't quite read your writing.'

'That's all right. I remember now. What about Saturday?'

'Tell you what. I'll talk to you again tomorrow, and I'll fill you in on your Saturday schedule then.'

'Brett!'

'If you change your mind about coming to Chicago, let me know.'

'I won't.'

'I told you, no hanky-panky. I don't set out to corrupt news people, just inform them.'

'I'm staying here, Brett. Can I at least have your phone number?'

'Why? Don't you trust me to call you?'

'Do you really want me to answer that?'

'I don't think I'll give it to you. My secretary says I should be very careful of who has access to——'

'I'll just bet she does,' Rebecca said grimly. 'That lady takes very good care of you. Look after my bag, all right?'

'Certainly. Is locking it in my safe with the secret formulas good enough, or would you prefer me to carry it everywhere I go? I'm sure it would raise a few eyebrows, but for you, nothing is too much trouble. I'll talk to you tomorrow, Rebecca.'

In the next few days, she learned what inconvenience was. She hadn't realised how many of her possessions had found their way into her handbag and stayed, until she tried to sew on a button, file her fingernails, and cure the headache brought on by the whole mess. Only then did she remember that her sewing-kit, her last emery board, and her bottle of aspirin were in her bag, in Chicago. Along with heaven knew what else, she thought irritably, trying to remember what might be at the bottom of that handbag. If there was anything embarrassing or peculiarly personal to be found, she was certain that Brett Hilliard had discovered it by now.

'And damned foolish it was of you to give him a weapon like that,' she scolded herself. In fact, the only good thing she could find about the whole experience was that her apartment had got the most thorough cleaning it had had in months, as Rebecca searched every drawer, every container, and every piece of furniture for stray coins. She resurrected a grand total of eighty-seven cents, and she hoarded it like a miser.

She talked to Brett each evening, and he faithfully relayed her list of appointments for the next day. Each evening he also told her what he had done that day, and detailed his plans for the evening. Once it was dinner at a Rush Street restaurant, followed by dancing at a new nightclub.

'Does your secretary like to dance?' she asked spitefully.

'Oh, I'm not taking her out tonight,' he said airily. 'See? If you had only come up to get your bag, you'd be going with me.'

Rebecca sighed. It did sound inviting. Not Brett exactly, she told herself quickly, but the city—the atmosphere—the elegance.

'I'd much rather have you,' he said. He sounded a little wistful, as if he really meant it.

She gave him points for the act. 'I'm sure you have no lack of females to choose from,' she said.

'Well, no. I do like variety, now and then. Don't you?'

'I am engaged, you know.'

'That's true. And you've made a good choice.'

'Oh? I thought you didn't like Paul.'

'I don't. But if you're looking for a lack of variety——'

She hung up on him. He promptly called back. 'You forgot to ask about your appointments,' he chided. 'Sometimes I think my secretary was right—you did the whole thing on purpose just so you could talk to me.'

'I didn't ask you to call me every day! Why are you doing this, anyway? You must have better things to do with your time than to call me!'

'I can't think of a single one. Actually, I enjoy talking to you when you're being human.'

It made her furious. 'I suppose you're doing it because it tickles you to think that I spend all my time sitting beside the phone waiting for you to call. Well, I'm not! I'm at home because I don't have a car and I can't afford to go anywhere—and don't you think it has anything to do with you, except that you're being a miserable, mean slob not to give me my purse back——' She was almost sobbing.

He clucked soothingly. 'Are you certain I'm not doing you a service? Who would you get mad at if you didn't have me to yell at once a day?' He didn't give her a chance to answer. 'You keep a horrid schedule, Rebecca.' She could hear pages turning. 'I always thought radio people had an easy life. You sit around for a couple of hours a day and chatter, and draw a big cheque. But the pay isn't so glamorous either, is it?'

She sniffed angrily. 'The amount I'm paid is my business, Brett—not yours.'

'It's not exactly confidential information when I have your latest cheque. Don't get ice cubes in your voice when you talk to me, Rebel. Paul might let you get by with it, but I won't.'

'My name is Rebecca. The programme director thought Rebel had a better sound on the air.'

'I happen to think he was inspired, but let's not argue about it. How long has Paul known you, anyway? Were you babies in the cradle together?'

'No. I knew him in school, of course, but he was a couple of years ahead of me. I didn't date him then, if that's what you're asking. Why? Do you think it's really any of your business?'

'And he hasn't realised yet that you're really Rebel underneath? Or don't you show him that side? He may have known you for a long time, but I suspect he doesn't know you very well.'

'What makes you say that?' She was stung, as well as curious.

'Because you just can't stay out of controversy. You aren't going to be very successful as Caesar's wife, and somehow I think that's what Paul expects of you.'

'What business is it of yours?'

'None,' he said cheerfully. 'I just wondered if he was going to get an unpleasant shock as soon as the honeymoon is over.'

'Just give me my appointments, Brett.'

'Oh? You don't want Dr Hilliard's quick-fix psycho-analysis? Why don't you come up and we'll discuss it?' But he stopped teasing and read off her next day's schedule.

The following night he told her he was going to see the new smash comedy that had just left Broadway. When he mentioned that he had an extra ticket, Rebecca had to swallow hard to fight down the envy that swept over her. She loved plays, and she rarely got the chance to see good ones. 'And who is the lucky lady tonight? Your secretary?' she asked finally.

'You mustn't think that she's the only woman in my life, Rebecca.'

'How does she feel about the company moving, and leaving all the glitter of the city behind?'

'Oh, she's in favour. She thinks it will be good for business.'

'I suppose she thinks it will cut down on the competition for you, too,' Rebecca muttered snidely.

He didn't answer. She heard the rattle of paper as he turned pages in her appointment calendar. 'You're supposed to go to the band concert with Paul tomorrow evening. Are your dates with him so easily forgettable that you have to write them down, Rebecca?' He sounded concerned. She wasn't impressed.

That was Sunday evening. She put the telephone down with a bang and decided that she needed some fresh air. She walked to the supermarket with her eighty-seven cents and in pure pique spent most of it on a chocolate bar—the biggest one she could find, and one produced by Brett's strongest competitor. She dropped the remaining pennies into the pocket of her white shorts and started for home, savouring the chocolate, nibbling a tiny bite and letting it melt on her tongue, then crunching the crisp almonds, and wishing that it was Brett she was crushing between her teeth.

It had become a matter of pride to her, to survive the weekend without borrowing money or begging rides. Besides, she admitted privately, she didn't want to admit to anyone just how embarrassing the whole thing was. Not even Gwen knew the worst of it; she assumed that once Rebecca knew for certain where her handbag was, there was nothing much left to be concerned about.

On Monday evening, the band concert started before dark, and when Paul came to pick her up, Brett had not yet made his regular call. Rebecca was torn between wanting to stay at home, in case there was something important on her calendar for Tuesday that she would forget about entirely if she wasn't reminded, and an irrational desire to hurry off to the concert to avoid the possibility that Brett would call while Paul was in the apartment. She wouldn't put it past him; after all, he did know the precise time Paul was to pick her up.

They walked from Rebecca's apartment down to the

central square, where the city band was arranged on the courthouse lawn. The fountain was spraying, the rush of water against the stone basin a soothing melody. As they walked across the grass, hand in hand, Paul said, 'I hate to bring up business on a beautiful night, but——'

'What is it?'

'Well, the payment on your car loan was due today.'

Rebecca stifled a groan. She had forgotten all about the car payment, because it was automatically deducted from her account each month. She hadn't given it a thought.

'And when the girls at the loan desk tried to withdraw the money from your account——'

'There wasn't enough there to cover it,' Rebecca agreed. 'Oh, damn.'

'They came to me, of course. Rebecca, it's so unlike you. You've never missed a payment before——'

'This is an unusual situation.'

'That's what everyone says the first time,' Paul muttered with sudden cynicism.

'Well, it is. And it isn't only the first time, it's the last time. I'll make a deposit Wednesday, without fail.'

'What's the matter, Rebecca? Did you buy something you couldn't afford? Lose money playing poker?'

He was trying to make a joke of it, she thought, even though it was a rather heavy-handed joke. 'Of course not,' she said. 'I just—well, I sort of lost track of my pay cheque.'

He stopped dead in the middle of the sidewalk. 'You what? Lost your cheque?'

'No—not exactly. I know where it is, it's just that I can't get it back and deposit it till Wednesday. If you could just explain to the loan people that I'm not defaulting——'

'Rebecca, I can't make a habit of this,' he warned.

'You said yourself I've never missed a payment before!'

'Just because I'm employed at the bank doesn't mean that you can rely on me to cover things up.'

'I am not asking you to conceal anything! I just want two days' grace on my car payment this month, all right?'

'I'll have to check it out with my father.'

'Oh, Paul, for heaven's sake. You're a vice-president.'

'And that means that I have to be exceptionally careful. Do you know how closely the bank inspectors watch my own accounts? You'll have to be more careful, Rebecca.'

'Caesar's wife?' she muttered. It was an unpleasant echo of what Brett had said.

'Laugh about it if you like, but they're very touchy about anything of this sort. The idea that I've shifted money to cover a customer's accounts, or made special arrangements——'

'Don't expect me to believe that, Paul. Bankers make special arrangements all the time.'

'Well, my father wouldn't like it very well.'

'He will only have to put up with it till Wednesday. And I'll pay a penalty, if that would help soothe him——'

I can't believe we're saying these things, she thought. What was it Brett had said—you can always borrow money from your boyfriend, if you have collateral? It seemed he had been right.

Oh, come on, she told herself. Of course Paul was careful; some people did think that being friends with a banker meant that they didn't have to worry about balancing their accounts any more. There were probably women who thought if they married a banker, they had an unlimited supply of cash . . .

Well, not me, Rebecca thought. And it makes me angry that Paul seems to think I'm like that.

'I've told you before that you should just arrange to have your cheque automatically deposited,' Paul said.

She couldn't resist. 'I still wouldn't have had any money this week,' she said. 'I don't have my cheque book either.'

He looked stunned, but the concert started then, and he was forced to lapse into silence. It was just as well, Rebecca thought. She didn't exactly want to discuss her feelings with Paul in a public place.

By the time the concert was over, though, she had cooled off. Paul was only watching out for his job; she couldn't exactly blame him for that. And since she would never be late with a car payment again, the problem would never come up again. Why waste time arguing about it? Besides, she decided, right now it was far more important that they talk about Cleo, and get a wedding date set.

He bought her a cone at the ice-cream shop on the corner of the town square and walked back to Rebecca's apartment through the dusk. She took a big bite of double chocolate almond and let it melt in her mouth, the cold liquid soothing her throat. 'Paul,' she said finally. 'Your mother seems to think that our wedding is going to include more people than the entire Hundred Years' War. I think we should decide some things soon.'

'Such as?' He had started on his second dip.

'Such as when we're getting married, and how many people to invite. It's a small church, honey, and I think about two hundred people will be the limit.'

'Rebecca, my mother has more old friends than that.'

'I know. I'm afraid that's going to be the problem. I thought the only fair thing to do was to tell her soon that her half of the guest-list will be limited to a hundred people.'

'I thought you meant two hundred for her.'

'There will be a few people I want to invite to my wedding,' she said, with a twinge of sarcasm. 'Do you suppose you could tell her that? Make her understand that she'll simply have to cut her list?'

He crunched his cone, and said. 'There is an easier solution. Instead of getting married in your church, which is admittedly small, we could have the ceremony at ours. It seats nearly a thousand, Rebecca. It would make it much easier.'

'I don't want to be married in an echoing tomb——'

'It will scarcely echo when it is full of people.'

'But that's the point, Paul. Don't you see? It's the most important day of my life, and I want to have the people who mean the most to us there—not everyone our parents owe social debts and political favours to!'

'You'll have those people. You'll just have a few extras.' He carefully folded the paper that had protected his cone from drips, and put it in a rubbish bin on the pavement.

'I have never considered being married anywhere except in my own church, Paul.'

'What's the big deal? It's not as if we're of different faiths, or something. It's just neighbourhood boundaries. You'll be going to services in the big church after we're married, so why not have the wedding there?'

She struggled for a way to explain it to him. What made it difficult was that everything Paul said made sense. It was just that she was convinced it wasn't right for her, and explaining that to him would be the hard part.

They stopped at the gate. 'Want to come up?' she said.

'Sure.' He smiled. 'I can't say a proper goodnight to my girl in public, can I?'

As they climbed the porch steps, a voice from the darkness said, 'Well, at last you've come home.'

'Brett!' Rebecca exclaimed. 'You weren't supposed to be here till tomorrow!'

Beside her, Paul tensed, and Rebecca would have liked to bite her tongue out on the spot. She could almost feel the questions coursing through him—why was Brett Hilliard here, and how did Rebecca know what his schedule was? And even though she was completely innocent, Rebecca felt her cheeks begin to burn in the darkness.

'Hello, Paul.' The deep voice was polite, but no more.

'Hilliard.' Paul sounded stiff.

Rebecca could hear the smile in Brett's voice; she had had plenty of practice in the last few days. 'I was just returning Rebecca's lost property,' he said gently.

'Oh. I'd almost forgotten.' Rebecca reached for the handbag.

Brett refused to let it go. 'I have been sitting here for quite a while, waiting for you,' he pointed out. 'A glass of iced tea or something would be quite welcome.'

'You've probably been here for all of five minutes,' Rebecca snapped. 'And it's your own fault, anyway, if you've had to wait. You knew when I'd be here——' She tried to bite the word off in the middle, and knew it was too late.

'Oh?' Paul asked sternly. 'And how did he know that? Have you and Mr Hilliard made plans, Rebecca?'

'Of course not. For heaven's sake, Paul, I didn't even know he was coming back tonight. How could we have had plans?'

'Then how did he know when you'd be home?'

'Would you keep your voice down, please?'

'Am I embarrassing you, Rebecca?'

Brett intervened. 'If we could just step inside, Rebecca, I'm certain I could explain this to Paul's satisfaction.'

'If you'd just give me my handbag and go away, I'd explain it myself.'

He didn't seem to hear, and a moment later she gave up. 'All right,' she said crossly, and fished her borrowed apartment key out of her pocket. 'You could have just let yourself in and left the damned bag,' she muttered to Brett as they climbed the walnut staircase to her door.

'He has a key to your apartment?' Paul was horrified.

'Haven't you got the message yet? He had my handbag, Paul—he's not only got my keys, he has my life story.'

Paul shook his head. 'You're becoming very careless, Rebecca.'

'And don't think I haven't learned my lesson,' she snapped.

Brett smiled. 'I thought about picking up your mail,' he said, 'but I didn't know which post-office box I had the key for. Besides, I thought perhaps you'd rather do it yourself.'

'You can say that again. If you two would like to make yourselves comfortable in the living-room and hash out your little explanations, I'll bring you lemonade.' As soon as the shouting dies down, she told herself morosely.

She had made one little careless mistake, and it looked as if she was going to be paying for it forever. Brett thought it was funny, and Paul considered it a tragic flaw in her character. But it was apparent that neither of them was going to let her forget it.

By the time she brought three large glasses of lemonade to the living-room, the conversation had settled down to inanities about the weather and the town. Brett, she thought, seemed to be enjoying it, as if he was playing cat-and-mouse. Paul was sitting stiffly on the edge of a chair. Rebecca wanted to pour the lemonade over both their heads and run.

'I noticed, as I was waiting on the porch,' Brett said, 'that this seems to be a very well-kept-up house.'

'I have a good landlord,' she said. 'The rent is reasonable, he repairs things almost before they break, and he lets his tenants paint the rooms any colour they like—as long as it's off-white.'

'Most of them do that,' Brett said. 'I can see why. You like it here, then?'

'Of course.' Idle conversation is the most sickening invention of humankind, she thought. We sound like a bunch of strangers at a cocktail party.

'It's getting late,' he said, and stood up. 'I'm sure you're anxious to be alone. Thank you for the lemonade, Rebecca.'

She followed him to the door, not out of politeness, but because she wanted to be certain that he left. He had accomplished what he had intended, she was sure—he had planted a very large doubt in Paul's mind. 'Why did you come back early?' she asked.

He smiled. 'Can't you guess?'

'I haven't a clue,' she said tartly, and wished, when she saw the gleam in his eyes, that she had never asked.

'I missed you,' he said. 'And sparring on the phone just wasn't good enough. I wanted to look at your lovely face, and touch your silky skin, and kiss your soft lips——' His mouth brushed hers, so lightly that it was like a butterfly's caress. Then he smiled down into her eyes and flicked her cheek with a gentle finger. 'You're not meant for Paul, you know. You never were. Goodnight, dear. See you at the council meeting tomorrow.'

CHAPTER FIVE

THE City Council met as scheduled on Tuesday, argued for the better part of the day, and adjourned without a decision on the Hilliard Confectioners question. Rebecca considered that their refusal to act was a moral victory for her. She didn't hesitate to say so at the end of that day's *Rebel with a Cause*, when she reminded her listeners that the next day Brett Hilliard himself would be her guest.

Gwen was waiting for her in the reception-room, where she had listened to the show over the speaker mounted high on the wall. 'Good grief, Rebecca,' she said, without even a hello. 'Don't you have any more sense than to call the man a liar on the air? That's slander, to start with, and——'

'I didn't call him anything.'

'I won't be surprised if you get beaten up some night in a dark alley,' Gwen said fatalistically. 'And don't come crying to me when it happens.'

'It won't happen, Gwen.'

'Why are you so sure? Because he's a gentleman?'

'No. Because he's got much more effective ways of dealing with opposition than that,' Rebecca said, without stopping to think about what she was saying.

'Would you listen to yourself? You're daring him, do you know that, Rebecca? He's going to retaliate.'

'He can't possibly do anything until the shouting about the plant is over. And then he'll probably slink quietly back to Chicago and that's the last we'll see of Mr Brett Hilliard.' Funny, she thought, that it wasn't an inviting idea.

'You don't think he'll vanish that easily, do you?'

72

'Gwen, did you come downtown to help me plan a wedding, or to lecture me about Brett?'

Gwen grinned. 'Actually, I came because it was a wonderful excuse to hire a babysitter and get away from the kids.'

A bellboy from the hotel across the square came in with a big box. 'Package for Miss Barclay,' he told the receptionist. Janet pointed at Rebecca, and the bellboy came across the room to her. 'I was to give it to you personal, he said.'

Rebecca frowned. 'Who said?'

'Mr Hilliard. He said to be sure you and nobody else got it.'

She took the box, half afraid of the contents. 'Well thank you—I think.'

'Oh, it was my pleasure, miss.' He grinned, and confided, 'The gentleman tips real nice.'

'I'm not surprised,' she murmured and started to strip off the paper. 'Is it a bomb, do you suppose?'

'I shouldn't think so,' Gwen said cheerfully. 'He'd hardly have had time to assemble one.'

The paper slipped off, revealing a gold foil box with an embossed label. 'Chocolates,' Rebecca said. 'Sweets to the sweet? Do you think that's what he meant?'

'I doubt it, considering what you just said about him. Is there a note?'

Rebecca inspected the wrapping paper. 'Nothing.'

'Hmmm.' Gwen gazed thoughtfully at the top layer of candies.

Rebecca laughed. 'Don't worry, Gwen. Everything but the caramels should be safe—he knows those are my favourites.'

Gwen shrugged and took a cream-centred candy. 'I'll try my luck,' she said. 'What the heck? We only live once, and if a woman has to go, eating poisoned Hilliard chocolates isn't a bad way.'

'I wonder if he carries boxes of these around with him.'

'If you ever manage to strike up a civil conversation with the man, you can ask him,' Gwen recommended indistinctly.

That was patently unfair, Rebecca thought. They had had several civil conversations on the telephone, but of course, Gwen didn't know about that.

She wrapped the box up again and asked Janet to keep it for her. 'I'll put it in your desk,' the girl said. 'I wouldn't be able to stand it with them in view—I adore Hilliard chocolates, and I can never afford them.'

'Help yourself,' Rebecca told her. 'Eat all you like.'

'But inspect them carefully for hypodermic needle marks,' Gwen warned. 'Where to, little sister?' she asked as they reached the street. 'Florists? Photographers? Printers? Or are we shopping for dresses today?'

'Cleo seems to think I'll have a second-rate wedding because I can't have a dress specially designed in time.'

'Poor Cleo. You mean that you've set a date?'

'Well—we can't, actually, until we've decided where the ceremony will be. But we thought December the first would be nice.'

'If you insist.' Gwen was not enthusiastic.

'I thought you liked the idea of a winter wedding.'

There was a long silence. Then Gwen said, 'It's not the season that bothers me, Rebecca. It's just that—oh, honey, be sure that you're doing the right thing. Marriage is tough enough in the best of circumstances, but——' She smothered what sounded almost like a sob.

'It's not going well between you and Bill, is it?'

'Is it that obvious? No, it's not.'

They walked along in silence for a few minutes. I don't know what to say, Rebecca thought, and found herself wishing that her mother was still alive. Mom would know just how to get Gwen to talk, she told herself. 'Is it another woman?'

'Oh, heavens, no. Unless you count his business— it's a more demanding mistress than any woman could be. Sometimes, Rebecca, I feel like going out and having a fling just to see if Bill would even notice that I was gone. If it wasn't for the kids——'

'Gwen, I had no idea. But he loves you, I'm sure of it——'

'He has a funny way of showing it,' Gwen said. 'I should have married someone like Brett. There's never any doubt about him.'

Was Gwen working herself up to have an affair? Or, Rebecca wondered uneasily, had she and Brett already picked up where they had left off in their college days? If so, was this Gwen's effort to excuse her behaviour?

Not my sister, Rebecca told herself. I've never seen anything that was the least bit suspicious.

And not Brett, she thought. He couldn't say the things he does to me if he was even contemplating sleeping with my sister. She's a married woman——

And you're an engaged one, she reminded herself, and that hasn't stopped him for a moment.

'Have you been seeing a lot of Brett?' she asked.

'Quite a bit, yes.' Gwen sounded carefully casual. 'You didn't tell me what we were shopping for today. Where do we start?'

And that, Rebecca thought, is that. She's not going to say another word. 'Let's stop at the drugstore first; I need some freckle cream.'

'I thought I just gave you a big tube.'

'You did. It's the only thing that was missing when I got my handbag back.'

Gwen giggled. Rebecca thought it sounded a little forced. 'Well, it did say on the label that it was vanishing cream!'

'At least, it was the only thing I've missed for certain,' Rebecca added, 'though I get the feeling that there were some other things there too; I just can't remember what. It's incredibly frustrating not to *know*. As far as that goes, I'm not absolutely certain the tube was in there. Really,

Gwen, why he would take a tube of freckle cream?'
Rebecca wrinkled her nose. 'Though, to be perfectly
fair——'

'You? Fair to Brett Hilliard? Ha!'

Rebecca ignored her. 'He did tuck a handful of
chocolates into my make-up bag.'

'Nice man to know,' Gwen said. 'It's probably
fortunate for me that I'm going home in a few weeks, or
I'd weigh a trillion pounds.'

So he was giving Gwen chocolates too? Rebecca
caught herself up short in the middle of the thought. In
the first place, why shouldn't he? And in the second
place, what did it matter?

I'm concerned about my sister, she told herself grimly.
And that's all I'm worried about.

'Gwen, this is not getting my shopping done.'

'How can you make any decisions when you're not
even certain of the wedding day?'

'I can't. But I want to find out what it's going to cost.'

'More than you can believe,' Gwen said, with the voice
of experience. 'Weddings cost twice as much as you plan
for; that's a law of nature. But Dad will help.'

'Are you positive about that? He's scarcely speaking to
me.'

'Well, he isn't very happy with you about the Hilliard
affair. But surely it will have all died down by then.'

'Oh, I know he won't exactly disown me. But it's my
wedding, Gwen, and I've been on my own for years. I
don't want Dad to have to bail me out.'

'Then you'd better put the brakes on Cleo right away.'

'Why do you say that?'

'Because Dad and I had dinner at the country club last
night, and she and Paul's father were there. She brought
her coffee over to our table, sat down, and told Dad that
it was very important to give two young people the
correct start in life. Which, in Cleo's terms, apparently

means the most lavish wedding since Napoleon married what's-her-name.'

'Josephine?'

'No, the other one. You know history was never my strong point. Cleo was discussing—with great insight, I thought—the things to be considered in choosing a vintage French champagne——'

'Oh, no.'

'——to wash down the Russian caviar. I can't remember which brand of caviar she recommended, but it stuck in my mind that she thought it would take at least a dozen cases of champagne.'

'It's easy to spend other people's money, isn't it?'

'Darling, what do you expect from a banker's wife?'

'Actually, I was thinking in terms of strawberry punch and some nice little tea sandwiches and a couple of kinds of cake——'

Gwen shook her head. 'Good luck.'

'Dammit, Gwen, it's my wedding. I should be able to have what I want!'

'You'll get no argument from me about that. I think if you want to get married in the middle of your radio show it should be entirely up to you. And the groom, of course; it might be wise to consult him about it. But you'd better get ready for a fight, because Cleo is not going to give in easily.'

'Well, she'll just have to,' Rebecca said firmly. 'I'm not going to be bullied.'

But the fun had gone out of the shopping-trip. When Rebecca looked at photographs, she thought of the size of album that Cleo would be likely to want. When she asked about cakes, she found herself giving the number of guests that Cleo wished to invite. When she browsed through the bridal shop's catalogues, she wondered which patterns Cleo would think appropriate for a banker's bride.

Maybe I should just give in, she thought. After all, a

wedding was only one day out of an entire lifetime. Wasn't it more important to lay a foundation of co-operation for the future? She would have to get along with Cleo for the rest of her life. There was no sense in making it harder by arguing about things that really didn't matter. If Cleo wanted a society wedding—well, what was the big deal? Plenty of girls would kill to be in Rebecca Barclay's shoes—to be treated like a queen on her wedding day.

But when the florist asked about her choice of colours, and she said, without thinking, 'Red and Cleo,' she found herself wondering where it would all end.

It was ten minutes to air time, and Rebecca was beginning to be concerned. Neither Brett nor her father had turned up yet, and it was beginning to look as if—for the first time ever—*Rebel with a Cause* had been stood up by a scheduled guest.

She poked her head into Janet's office. 'Have you seen my guests?' she asked, knowing that it was a useless question. If they had arrived, Janet would have called her to come and get them—or else Rebecca would have run into them on her way from the broadcast-booth to the office.

'Yes. Didn't you see them? They're in the station manager's office.'

'He hijacked my guests?'

'He said it would only take a little while. Jack Barnes is in there, too, so he'll get them back to you in time.'

'The time,' Rebecca noted, 'is five minutes to air.'

'Want me to call him on the intercom and remind him?'

'No. That would probably only slow things down. If they haven't come out in a couple of minutes, though——'

Janet nodded. 'I'll knock on the door and tell Jack the building is on fire. Here—take this candy out of my office would you, Rebel? I can't get my mind off it today, and I think I've gained five pounds just by looking at it.'

Rebecca was passing the station manager's office when the door opened. 'Happy to do anything I can,' the manager was saying, as he shook hands with the Mayor. 'This town needs economic development.'

Brett had seen her. 'Miss Barclay doesn't seem to agree,' he said mildly.

'Shall we discuss it on the air?' she asked sweetly.

He didn't answer. 'I'm glad to see you're on time today.'

'I am always on time,' she pointed out. 'If you're talking about the television show last week——'

'I was.'

'It isn't my fault if someone told you to come early.'

He didn't comment; she couldn't tell if he believed her. 'I see you finally got your box of chocolates.'

'I wonder why you sent it,' she mused. She showed the two of them into the broadcast-booth, closed the soundproof door, and indicated the two chairs across from the control-panel. 'Make yourselves comfortable.'

The Mayor rummaged through the foil box of candy and found a cherry cordial.

'Bribery won't get you anywhere with me,' she added. She began flipping switches and stacking cartridges of commercials and features in the order in which they would be used.

The Mayor sighed, as if his worst fears about the afternoon were beginning to come true.

Brett's dark eyebrows arched in astonishment, and he said, sounding shocked, 'Bribery? I certainly intended nothing of the sort, Rebecca.'

'Of course not,' she said cynically. 'I'm sure it was intended as a thank-you!'

'As a matter of fact,' he said, sounding quite serious, 'it was.'

'I'll bet,' she said. 'By the way, there is a tube of freckle cream missing from my handbag.' She tipped her head defiantly and glared at him.

'I know,' he said easily. 'I like your freckles just the way they are. I like all of you, just the way you are.'

That left her staring at him in astonishment for a moment, before she shook her head and went back to putting her notes in order. It was obvious that she shouldn't fence with him, she thought. Brett Hilliard had turned flirting into an art form.

She slipped on her headphones, so that she could hear what the disc jockey in the adjoining control-room was saying, and just as the sweep second-hand marked two o'clock, she flipped the lever that put her microphone on the air. She and the DJ exchanged a bit of patter, and then *Rebel with a Cause* began for another day.

Ted Barclay, she noted, was nervous as he waited to be introduced. He was tugging at his tie and toying with the paper wrappers that had held chocolates in the foil box. Brett Hilliard, on the other hand, sat quietly, perfectly at ease, his big brown eyes intent on every move of her hands as she played with the control-board.

'Dad, please,' she said, during the theme music, while her microphone was dead. 'That paper rattles, and it sounds like static on the air.'

'Sorry, Rebecca.' He pushed the chocolate box away. 'I'm just like a kid when it comes to candy.'

'That explains a few things,' she murmured. The theme music came to an end, and her microphone was live. She introduced her guests, reminded her callers of the telephone number, and turned to Brett. 'Mr Hilliard, let's talk about your plans for Hilliard Confectioners——'

'Now that we know each other so much better, Miss Barclay, why don't you call me Brett?'

There was nothing actually off-colour about the suggestion. And yet it made her uneasy, as if he had implied that they knew each other very, very well.

She didn't want to do it; she would much rather remain
formal with guests on the show, but she couldn't think of
a polite way to refuse. 'All right, Brett. And I'm Rebel—
on the air.'

'Only on the air?' he murmured.

She could see his strategy now. Get her off balance
with these personal remarks, and she couldn't concentrate on the real topic. Well, he would soon learn that
tactics like that didn't affect Rebel Barclay!

'Brett, tell us why you feel it's necessary for the city to
put up a building, give you land, and absorb all of these
expenses——'

'Rebel——' There was emphasis on the name. 'The
city isn't giving me anything. The council is considering
making me a loan, in effect. It's a loan that will be repaid
in cash eventually and by community development
almost immediately.'

'Interest-free,' Rebecca put in smoothly. It was
impossible, she thought, to stir him to anger, and she had
to admire his control. 'Why the need for the loan?' she
asked.

'It is massively expensive to relocate a corporation of
this size.'

'Your company is very profitable.'

'Making a profit is not a crime,' he said. 'Let's face it,
Rebel, if this station didn't make a profit, it couldn't stay
in business, and you wouldn't have a job.'

'You haven't answered my question. Why should
Fultonsville pay the bill to move your company here?'

'Financially, Hilliard Confectioners would be far
better off in the short term to rebuild the existing plant.
In the long view, of course, the new location is our best
guess for a profitable future. But the company does
assume an enormous risk in making a move of this
sort——'

'A risk?' she interrupted. 'Does that mean that you've
prepared an escape plan in case this experiment isn't a

success? And what happens to the city's money if it isn't? Have you shared that information with the City Council, Brett?'

'The City Council, being a group of reasonable men and women, know that economic development doesn't come with a guarantee. But we certainly do not have an escape plan. We want this to work, just as much as everyone in Fultonsville does—with the possible exception of you.'

'That's simply not true,' she interrupted. 'I've talked to dozens of people in this town who are afraid of this project. They're all for economic development, but the risks are too much for them——'

He overrode her protest. 'Frankly, Rebel, I'm getting a little tired of your assumption that I'm looking for a way to cheat this city. I certainly have nothing to gain from moving my company down here and then leaving town. On the contrary, I would have a great deal to lose.'

The phone lines were lighting up. This was going to be a good show, she thought; it was obvious that the citizens had questions.

The first call, however, startled her. 'I've listened to your show for a long while, Rebel,' the caller said. She recognised the voice; it was a middle-aged man who called about once a week, and whose opinions were always cogent and usually tart. 'But this is the first time I've been embarrassed to be a fan of yours. If you aren't careful, they're going to rename your show—and call it Dial-a-Dummy.'

'I don't think it will go that far,' Brett put in.

She glared at him. If there was one thing she didn't need right now, it was Brett coming to her rescue!

The caller went on, 'Be reasonable, Rebel. This is the best chance Fultonsville's got. Can't you see that? Of course there are no guarantees. Did you ever think about a raccoon that's being chased by a hound dog?'

'No,' Rebecca said. 'I don't quite see what that has to do with this——'

'Didn't expect you would. The raccoon's got a choice to make. He can either duck and weave and run like crazy and maybe get to safety up a tree somewhere, or he can sit still and wait for the dog to catch him. Now running isn't guaranteed to save his life—he may use every trick he knows and every bit of breath he's got and still get caught. But at least he's tried.'

'And that's the position this town's in now,' Ted Barclay put in. 'Is that what you mean?'

'That's right, Your Honour. For the last two or three years we've just been sitting still, waiting for the hound to catch up. Now it's time for some fancy footwork. We may not get away clean, but at least we'll have tried.'

'Well, thank you for calling,' Rebecca said. 'An original philosophy,' she added, as she reached for the next phone call.

'That's one of the things I like best about this town,' Brett said. 'It has a homey atmosphere.'

'That's right,' the Mayor said. 'You'll be looking for a house, too, won't you?'

'Please, Your Honour,' Rebecca said. 'This is not an estate agent's. Let's stick to the business at hand.' She pushed the button for the next caller.

The woman burst into speech. 'Didn't anyone ever teach you respect, young woman?' she said. 'That's not what I called to say, but hearing you talk to your father like that, after all the good things he's done for this town, is enough to make my skin crawl.'

Rebecca had been looking down at the control-panel, where her list of questions to ask Brett lay on the ledge. One of the nicest things about radio, she had always thought, was the freedom it included. She didn't even have to maintain eye contact with her guest, as was so important in television.

Now, however, she found herself looking up at Brett.

What an odd thing to do, she thought, even as she did it. If she had glanced at her father, to see what effect that accusation had on him, that would have made sense. But to look at Brett——

He looked relaxed, but she wasn't fooled by that. She knew him well enough by now to know that he was coiled, ready to strike, no matter how indolent his pose. And in his dark eyes, there was a look of—was it concern? Of course not, she told herself. It wouldn't be that, it couldn't. He might be laughing at her, or glad to see her getting taken down a peg, but not concerned . . .

From there, the show turned into a rout. One caller asked about Hilliard Confectioners' civic projects, and Brett sent a small smile at Rebecca before he detailed the company's gifts to arts and sciences, to museums, to special fund drives. If she hadn't recognised the caller's voice, and known it was one of her regulars, she would have accused Brett of planting a public relations stunt.

It was uncomfortable. They didn't even talk during the commercial breaks. Rebecca kept her eyes on the control-panel and the log that showed her which advertisement was to play next. Ted Barclay stared at the wall and drummed his fingers on the table. Brett showed no sign of discomfort at all.

Each time Rebecca answered a call, it was with the hope that someone would back her up, that someone would question the sense of this move. Now and then someone did, but the protests were minimal. The majority of Fultonsville, it seemed, supported the plan. Where, she asked herself, are all the people I've been talking to for weeks?

Ted Barclay pointed that out in his closing remarks. 'The council will be delighted to hear how many people are firmly behind this project,' he said.

'Perhaps the ones who are opposed went out of town today,' Rebecca said tartly, and instantly regretted that she had allowed the words to cross her lips.

'If the numbers had run in the other direction, would you have said that?' Brett asked sweetly.

'Don't forget that the council vote hasn't been taken yet,' she pointed out.

Brett smiled, as if to say that he had no doubt of the outcome. But he was too smart, she saw with regret, actually to say anything that might be interpreted as over-confidence. Instead, he said, just as she started the music that signalled the end of the show, 'I'll make a very strong effort to change your mind this weekend, Rebecca.'

She stared at him for a moment, and then dismissed it. He had seen a chance to get in the last jab, and he had done it. He was probably hoping that Paul was listening to the show. Well, she decided, the best way to handle Brett Hilliard was to ignore him altogether.

As soon as she had closed down the control-panel, Ted Barclay stood up. With an expansive grin on his face, he slapped Brett on the back and said, 'I certainly didn't expect it to go like that! Congratulations, my boy.'

Sudden suspicion burned in her. 'Did you stack my show, Dad?'

'What?' He sounded honestly amazed.

'Arrange for sympathetic callers to keep the lines tied up, that's what I mean. Did you?'

'Cross my heart, Rebecca, I didn't do a thing. I don't play dirty politics.'

She turned to Brett. 'Then it was you. I wouldn't put anything past you.'

'Why are you so certain that someone tampered with the show? It's difficult to be a rabble-rouser when there isn't a base to work with, isn't it?'

'I am not a rabble-rouser.'

'Of course you aren't,' he said agreeably, in a tone that left no doubt as to his real convictions. 'You were well named, Rebecca.'

Now what on earth did that mean? she wondered. She

pushed the question aside as the two men left the broadcast-booth. It didn't matter, and in any case, he was gone now. She didn't have to deal with him ever again.

Her purpose had been achieved; she had asked the tough questions and had encouraged others to do the same. If no one responded to that prodding, it wasn't her fault. The City Council's decision, she thought, was a foregone conclusion now. If there was no disagreement on her show, then there was little in the town. Her father had been right about that much. And she knew better than to think the outcome could have been arranged.

She closed the room and left it ready for the next use, and started down the hall towards the exit. She was physically drained and ready to go home. There was work to be done in her office, but she was in no shape to do it.

I'll come in early tomorrow, she thought. There will be plenty of time to do everything tomorrow.

Jack Barnes was in the hallway, hovering just outside the television studio. A red light above the door warned that taping was in progress.

'The station manager wants to see you,' he said.

'Me?'

'Is there anybody else walking down the hall?'

Oops, Rebecca thought. He was probably listening to the show, and he's already said that he's not pleased about my attitude towards Hilliard Confectioners. But surely, after the beating I took on my own show today, he's not going to fire me on top of it?

A warning, she thought. I'm going to get a warning to behave myself, and toe the mark on future political questions. She groaned inwardly. If there was one thing she did not feel like doing this afternoon, it was fighting for her freedom of expression with the station manager. And yet, she could not back down. If she couldn't be free to say what she thought on the show, then what good was it?

'Hope you haven't made any plans for the weekend,' Jack Barnes said. He sounded pleased.

The weekend? It brought an unpleasant echo to Rebecca's mind. Brett had said something about the weekend . . . She dismissed it irritably. That had been only a misplaced joke.

'What do you mean?' she asked.

'You're going out on assignment.'

'At least that means I'm not getting fired,' she said, with a determinedly cheerful note. 'Jack, can we stop playing Twenty Questions? Where am I going?'

He grinned. 'Lucky girl,' he said. 'I'm not supposed to tell you. The manager wanted it to be a surprise. But I'm sure it won't take all weekend to come up with the story. You'll have plenty of time to enjoy yourself in the city.'

'The city?' Pictures began to form in her mind. The station manager, shaking Brett's hand and saying, *Happy to do anything I can.* Brett himself, saying, *I'll make a very strong effort to change your mind this weekend* . . . Jack Barnes, saying, *Enjoy yourself in the city*——

'He wants me to go to Chicago?' she said weakly.

Jack nodded. 'To do an investigative piece on Hilliard Confectioners. At the invitation of the boss himself. Have a good time, Rebel.' He leered a little. 'I'll bet that guy intends to show you one.'

CHAPTER SIX

'YOU are joking, aren't you?'

It was not the first time Paul had asked the question. Rebecca had broken the news to him over dinner, at the tiny table in front of the wide windows in her living-room. They had been discussing it since they started to eat. Now, as Rebecca poured coffee, she said, once again, 'I'm perfectly serious, Paul. The station manager called me in and told me I'm going to Chicago tomorrow.'

'He ordered you to go, just like that?'

Rebecca would have preferred to leave the word 'ordered' out of it; though of course it had been an order, she didn't like thinking about it in quite that way. 'It's an assignment for the station, Paul. I do news stories now and then, you know.'

Paul stirred his coffee. 'I'm surprised he's sending you, the way you feel about Hilliard.'

'Perhaps that's exactly why he wants me to go.'

'I mean, everybody knows you're opposed to this thing. I can't think he'd want a story like that. He's in favour of it.'

'Paul, no matter what my personal convictions are, I will put together a fair report.'

'But you feel so strongly——'

'Yes, and on my show I express my feelings. That's the kind of show it is. But I'm also a reporter, and I know when to stick to the facts.'

'I'm still surprised that he'd send you.'

I'm not, she thought. And I don't dare tell Paul why I know.

She hadn't lied to Paul; she had just said nothing about

88

seeing Brett Hilliard coming out of the station manager's office before the show. She hadn't wanted to tell Paul that Brett had made some sort of deal with the man, and that he must have requested this assignment for her. She really had no proof of that, she told herself.

But she knew it was true. Brett had set her up for a purpose, she was certain of that, and she knew that at least part of that design was to cause conflict between her and Paul. Rebecca didn't intend to add to her own problems by falling into the trap and blurting it all out to Paul.

'It's a very appropriate story for me to do, anyway,' she said. 'With the political experience I have, you see— most of the other reporters at the station are newcomers to town. They don't understand the background of this problem.'

Paul was still looking thoughtful. 'Well, I suppose that makes sense,' he admitted.

'If you're concerned about me—about Brett, I mean——' She stumbled a little. 'I don't plan to spend any more time with him than I have to.'

'That's logical,' he said. 'Nobody could get upset about you doing the story; that's just part of your job. But you'll have to be careful about the rest. You wouldn't want talk to get started.'

And neither would you, she thought. But how on earth would anyone in Fultonsville hear about it, anyway? 'At least we didn't have any really important plans for the weekend.'

'You'll be gone all weekend? I thought you said you'd probably be back on Saturday.'

'I will. It was just a manner of speaking. A couple of days should be all the time I need, and I can catch the early train on Saturday.'

'You're not taking your car?'

'No. You know how much I hate driving in the city.'

He sounded doubtful. 'But how will you get around?'

'Last time I checked, they still had cabs in Chicago,' she teased.

'Well, I'm glad you won't be driving around the city alone,' he admitted. 'Still——'

'I'm a big girl, Paul. And this is my job.'

'I know. Are you sure you can't be back early? Mother told me to ask you over for dinner Friday evening.'

'Oh. I'm sorry to miss that, Paul. Next week, perhaps?' I really am sorry, she thought. The sooner she grew to be comfortable around Paul's parents, the better it would be for everyone. She started to gather the dishes together.

'She'll be disappointed,' Paul warned. 'She wanted to talk to you about the wedding plans, and the carriage house.'

'The which?'

'You know. The carriage house—our garage.'

She remembered it now. The Fredericks house was an enormous Victorian mansion, with a garage the size of an ordinary two-storey house nestled behind it. Why, Rebecca wondered, would she want to talk to me about the garage? And why am I so certain I'm not going to like this topic?

'She's having such fun redecorating it,' Paul said. 'She's always wanted to use the top floor as a studio, you know——'

To do what? Rebecca thought rebelliously. She doesn't paint. She doesn't dance. She doesn't sculpt. She doesn't take photographs—why on earth would Cleo Fredericks want a studio? Then she answered her own question. Because, she thought, it would satisfy Cleo's sense of her own importance.

'But now she's making it into an apartment for us. It's providential, she says, that there is all that space just waiting for us. She's working very hard to be sure it will be ready by the time of the wedding.'

Rebecca stacked china with hands that were suddenly

shaky. 'And I suppose she wants to ask me about colours and things?'

He frowned. 'Oh, I don't think so. It looks as if she's got it pretty well arranged.'

Yes, Rebecca thought. Cleo would have. 'Paul—did you tell your mother we were going to live in the carriage house?'

He looked startled. 'Do you mean you don't want to? It's really going to be pretty.'

'I don't exactly mean that I don't want to live there,' Rebecca hedged. 'But I'd like to decide for myself. I'd like at least to see the place before it's decided.'

Paul's face tightened. 'Well, I've seen it. And I'm going to be living there too.'

She was instantly sorry. 'I didn't mean it that way, Paul. Of course we'll decide together. But I wish your mother hadn't gone to all this trouble before we even had a chance to think about where we want to live!'

'She only wants us to be comfortable, Rebecca. And happy. Why should we rent a tiny apartment somewhere when there's all that space going to waste?'

It made sense, and yet she was miserably uncomfortable. 'I never thought there was anything wrong with this apartment,' she pointed out softly.

Paul looked around. 'There isn't, really. And you've done a nice job. But you said yourself the other night that the landlord wouldn't allow you to paint it any colour but white. In the carriage house, we can have whatever we want. Show me another apartment in the whole town of Fultonsville that's being done by a decorator!'

She wanted to tell him that he'd hit on the problem precisely; Rebecca didn't want a decorator. She wanted her home to reflect her own tastes, not the shoulds and should-nots of a paid professional who had never even talked to her!

She looked around the living-room and sighed. Darkness was falling, and the candles on the table provided the only light in the apartment. Dusky shadows gathered in the corners of the room, making it seem like a cosy nest. The ruffled curtains at the windows played peek-a-boo with the dim moonlight, and the bright cushions piled on window seats and couches had mellowed with the change in light until they were deep jewel colours, inviting her to snuggle down in their comfort.

It had taken her four years to get this apartment just the way she liked it. She had assumed, since Paul was still living with his parents, that after the wedding he would move in with her, until they started their family and wanted to buy a house. Now——

'I'd like at least to look at it before we decide,' she said stubbornly.

'That's why Mother invited you for dinner on Friday,' Paul pointed out. 'But if you won't be in town——'

I could catch the commuter train back on Friday evening, she thought. No, even that would not get her into Fultonsville before ten at night. And the station manager had made it clear that he wanted a full report, not a sketch. She had better not skimp on the time she spent, or she would be in trouble all the way around. If Brett Hilliard was capable of setting this up, he certainly wouldn't hesitate to create more difficulties if she didn't do a thorough job.

'Saturday?' she suggested hopefully.

Paul shook his head. 'Mother and Dad have made plans. We'll look at next week's schedule, and I'll let you know.' His voice was precise and clipped as he said goodnight, and his kiss lacked its usual warmth.

Rebecca was miserable. I shouldn't have said anything at all, she thought. I should have just waited until I'd seen the place, and then if it was too impossible I could have talked to Paul about it. Now, I've caused trouble without even knowing if there is a problem. Nine chances out of ten, the apartment will be perfectly charming, and I'll fall

in love with it, and we'll have had this fight for
nothing——

Perfectly charming was one thing, though, she
thought, and living across the driveway from Cleo
Fredericks was another. She thought about that as she
prepared for bed, and scenarios flashed through her
mind one after another. Cleo, dropping in for coffee
regularly and without warning. Cleo, raising her eyebrows if Rebecca wasn't dressed to receive callers on
weekend mornings. Cleo, running a furtive finger over
the furniture to check for dust . . .

It's only upsetting you because you don't know her
very well yet, Rebecca told herself firmly. And besides,
those things could happen anywhere—whether you live
next door or two miles away.

She did not find the thought comforting.

She always enjoyed taking a train, even the commuter
trains that rattled and rocked and were noisy and grew
unpleasantly warm when the air-conditioning didn't
work quite properly. She liked to sit by the window and
look out dreamily as the countryside rolled past,
watching as river bluffs turned to meadows which turned
to hills which turned to towns, like the pieces of a crazy
quilt stitched together by a master hand. In the middle of
August, everything was green, and yet that didn't come
close to expressing what Illinois in the summer was like.
For there were so many shades of green. There was the
dark lush crispness of cornstalks stretching towards the
sky, reaching for moisture from the clouds that rolled by
unheeding. There was the blue-green of alfalfa, knee-
deep and heavily scented, waiting for the mowing-
machines to slice it away from the earth and turn it into
fodder for the winter. There were the last traces of pale
green in the golden oats, covering the fields in luxuriant
waves that rippled in the gentle breeze, nearly ready for
the harvest. And in the towns was the painter's green of

the lawns and the golf courses, spread out like carpets.

I haven't had time to play golf this summer, she thought. I wonder if Brett plays . . .

And why, she asked herself tartly, would she be wondering about him? If she wanted to play a round of golf, there were plenty of people to ask. Paul played at least once a week, with his father and a couple of the bank's biggest customers. Her father could be found on the course any afternoon when he wasn't at City Hall. Gwen even played once in a while, more for the walk than the game. But there was certainly no lack of partners.

I wonder if Cleo plays golf, Rebecca thought, or if she thinks it's unladylike.

'Oh, stop thinking about Cleo,' she muttered, 'and enjoy your trip.' Enjoy? she asked herself. Had she really said that? How perfectly ridiculous she was being today! As if a couple of days with Brett Hilliard could be anything but a nuisance.

She picked up her book and buried her nose in it, trying to stop thinking. But she found herself reading the same sentence over and over, as if she had never seen it before, and finally she put the book aside and leaned back in her seat, watching as small towns rolled by the window and joined together to form the outskirts of the city.

Perhaps, she decided, she should be glad of this trip. She hadn't been away from Fultonsville in months. 'You can get tunnel-vision,' she murmured, 'living in a small town.'

Perhaps that was what was wrong with Cleo, Rebecca thought; without enough things to keep her occupied, the woman had endless hours to find fault with others. And living across the driveway from her—that would be next to impossible, Rebecca told herself. The woman would practically feel obliged to keep Rebecca's house—and Rebecca herself—in line.

Don't jump to conclusions, she told herself firmly. You've never exactly felt like one of Cleo's favourites, but the only time the woman has actually been curt with you, you were late for lunch and you turned up covered with dust. No wonder she was less than pleased, but it doesn't mean she's going to try to take you over completely. Give her a fair chance, Rebecca.

The skyline of Chicago loomed against the brilliant blue. Rebecca retrieved her travelling bag from the rack above her seat and settled back to watch the city. She played the game of searching out favourite old landmarks, noting which towers had risen into view since her last trip, and mourning a few old favourites which had vanished.

I've missed the city, she thought.

The train pulled into the dark station-yard, and the lights in the cars brightened. Under the huge roof, it was like the middle of the night. The roar of the diesel engines was deafening as Rebecca walked up the platform to the bright doorway of the station itself.

Brett had come to meet her train. He was loitering just inside the terminal, reading the *Sun-Times*, when she came in. It didn't surprise her, and it didn't precisely please her, either, she told herself. 'Well,' she said. 'I am getting the celebrity treatment. Have you been waiting here all morning?'

He looked up with a smile, folded the newspaper under his arm, and took her carry-on bag from her hand. 'No. I read the timetable, and discovered that this is the only train that stops in Fultonsville. Is this all the luggage you have?'

She raised an eyebrow. 'I'm only staying a couple of days, Brett. I didn't think I'd need my entire wardrobe.'

'Then you're the most unusual woman I've ever met. Come on, let's get out of this confusion. Would you like an early lunch, or did you eat on the train?'

'There was a buffet car. Whether what it serves is

actually food is a matter of opinion.'

'In that case, we'll have lunch.'

'I think I'd rather get to work.'

He smiled. 'You'll need strength to work. And we can discuss chocolates over our coffee, if you insist.'

She decided there was no point in resisting. As a matter of fact, she hadn't eaten on the train. He was right; she could use the time to quiz him about the background of Hilliard Confectioners. Besides, she concluded, he had engineered this plot; let him pay the bill. It would be a tiny bit of revenge, at least.

He paused in the centre of the concourse. 'You didn't leave your handbag on the train, did you?' he asked solicitously.

She almost hit him with it, right there. 'You're never going to let me forget that, are you?'

His eyes were very bright. 'Never,' he agreed.

He took her to the Art Institute. She looked at the sleek, clean lines of the newer section of the museum, with its glass walls and modern sculpture, and said, 'I thought you said something about lunch. Or are you one of those who feel that good art is food for the soul?'

'Sorry to disappoint you, but my soul definitely comes after my stomach. You haven't been to the courtyard restaurant here? What a deprived childhood you've had, Rebecca.'

So now he had concluded that she was only a child, she thought. It was an irritating thought.

The courtyard was frantically crowded. Round tables, each topped with a bright yellow umbrella, surrounded a central pool with a fountain in the middle. Huge trees shielded the open court, and beyond them, through arched windows, art patrons could be seen now and then, strolling through the galleries.

The queue of people waiting for tables seemed to stretch for ever. Rebecca thought, we'll have to spend the afternoon queuing. Was that, she wondered, what he intended? It would certainly limit the time she had to look around at the factory.

But the woman who was working her way down the queue, telling one group after another that it would be nearly an hour until there was a place for them, paused and blinked when she reached Brett. 'Good morning, Mr Hilliard,' she said softly, without an instant's hesitation. 'We'll have a table for you in five minutes. Which side would you prefer?'

'The one farthest from the harpist,' he said, with a smile.

She smiled. 'She's good, really.' She went down the line, and Rebecca heard her tell a man behind them, 'About an hour and fifteen minutes, sir. I'll be happy to take your name, and if you'd like to look around the museum until then——'

'Are you so good at bribing people that no one can even spot the cash changing hands?' Rebecca asked softly. 'Or do you have special influence here?'

'It's called making reservations in advance,' he said.

'Oh. So even if I hadn't wanted lunch——'

He shrugged. 'You wouldn't like it if I starved to death at your feet this afternoon, would you?'

'I still think you bribed her. She didn't even have to ask your name.'

'Rebecca, your logic defies all reason.' He paused as the woman returned, and didn't speak again until she had taken them to a table at the far corner of the pool and given them menus. 'I could put so many holes in that statement that we could spend the entire weekend arguing about it. But I'd much rather talk about what we're going to do tonight.'

'Don't feel obliged to entertain me,' Rebecca said. 'I came up to do a story. I can fill up the rest of my time without help.'

He hadn't seemed to hear. 'I've got tickets to the play you wanted to see—the new comedy I told you about.'

She swallowed hard. He couldn't have presented her with a larger temptation if he had tailor-made it—which, she thought, he probably had. It must have been obvious in her voice, that night he had told her about the play, that she had wanted to go. 'But you've seen it,' she said.

He smiled, that heart-stoppingly warm, slightly crooked smile, and his voice was suddenly like the soft tones of an organ again. 'Only once,' he said. 'And it moves so quickly that by the time you finish laughing at one line, you've missed three more. I'm looking forward to seeing it again.'

She studied her menu, torn between her longing to see the show and her half-promise to Paul not to spend any time with Brett unless it was business.

Brett said, casually, 'If you don't want to do that, we can find something else. I've made plans for dinner, and afterwards we could go dancing, or something.'

She made up her mind. It was obvious that he intended to spend the evening with her, and while she could plead illness or lock herself in her hotel room and refuse to come out, what would she gain from such an exercise? Surely Paul would understand an evening spent at the theatre. She did have to co-operate with the man, after all, if she was to go home with a story.

Besides, she thought, the theatre would be a whole lot easier to explain to Paul than an evening spent dancing at a Rush Street nightclub, that was sure!

'The theatre sounds wonderful,' she said. 'If I can pay you for my ticket, that is.'

'I wouldn't hear of it.'

'It's a matter of ethics, Brett—a good reporter doesn't accept gifts from a source.'

He looked at her appraisingly, and then he smiled. 'In that case, of course you may pay for your ticket,' he said.

Rebecca hadn't expected him to give in quite so easily, and what should have felt like a victory instead left her feeling a bit apprehensive. He was watching her, she thought, like a cat who was stalking his prey. But she dismissed the feeling as they talked of art, of music, of the theatre.

'Gwen said you were both interested in the theatre when you were at the university.' She looked up at him cautiously. Would he give something away at the mention of Gwen's name?

'Yes, we were always hanging around the drama department.' It was easy, casual. 'I thought for a while that I wanted to be an actor.'

'Really? I assumed that chocolates had always been first in your life.'

He smiled. 'College drama was fun, but eventually the coach convinced me that since I had no talent I would starve to death trying to get to Broadway, so I finished my degree and came back to the family business.'

'I'll bet your father was pleased.'

'I thought for a while he might have bribed the drama coach to tell me I was hopeless, but he was actually very open-minded about it. He told me I couldn't be much of a candy-maker if my heart wasn't in it.'

'That's unusual.'

'Not if you knew my father. He's very young for his age. He's officially retired, but he's still on the board of directors, and he'd be in the thick of this if my mother hadn't dragged him off on a round-the-world cruise.' He sipped his coffee thoughtfully. 'By now he's probably led the crew into a mutiny.'

It was a shock to think of Brett with parents, or to consider what he might have been like as a boy. She didn't want to explore that any further. Instead, she said, 'There's a very good amateur theatre group in Fultonsville. You'd like it, I think.'

His eyes were suddenly brilliant. 'Do you know,' he mused, 'that's the first time you've sounded as if you wouldn't mind if I moved there.'

'Is it?' she said uncertainly. But I wouldn't mind, she

thought. It's certainly been a lot livelier place this summer——

Rebecca, she warned, don't you give in to his charm too!

'What about you?' he asked. 'Do you belong to the theatre group?'

She shook her head. 'I'm no actress. Gwen was in it for years, till she got married and moved.'

'Is it my imagination, or do we keep coming back to Gwen?'

'I guess I have her on my mind a lot just now.' Rebecca glanced up at him, and dropped her gaze back to the linen napkin she was pleating nervously. 'She's not very happy.'

'I know.' He sounded sombre. 'And until she figures out what she wants, no one can help her much.'

That's not much comfort, Rebecca thought. I wanted you to tell me that it doesn't matter to you what Gwen does. I wanted you to say that Gwen could go jump into the Mississippi River and you wouldn't care——

And what difference could it possibly make to me, she asked herself, and nearly choked on the answer.

Because you want him for yourself, she thought. You want him to care only about you . . .

That's ridiculous, she told herself. Utterly ridiculous.

'You should be a model,' he said, quite suddenly. 'The planes in your face——'

She laughed, a little nervously. 'You and Paul,' she said. 'He calls me a Titian redhead.'

Brett shook his head. 'Oh, no. You're far too slender for Titian's taste.'

The waiter put a plate before her, and Rebecca looked down at it and sighed. 'Not if you keep feeding me like this,' she said. 'I mean—I don't mean that I expect you'll take me out again——'

He laughed softly. 'Rebecca, you are so much fun to watch. You are so very obvious, my dear. Anything you feel washes straight up under that lovely transparent skin, and I can read it around the freckles——'

He brushed a gentle finger across her cheekbone, and she shivered. I hope he can't read my mind, she thought in fear. If he even suspects what was going through my mind just now——

He let his hand slip gently down a long lock of red hair that lay across her shoulder. 'And now you're shocked at me. Be a good girl and eat your chicken salad, and forget that I said anything at all,' he murmured.

But she couldn't forget that moment of blinding fear when she had realised that she wanted him for herself.

Rebecca was disappointed by her first view of Hilliard Confectioners. Even though he had told her about the old building, and the problems in the present location, she had still pictured it as a modern, sleek, up-to-date plant— something like Brett himself, she thought.

He seemed to read it in her eyes. 'Disappointing, isn't it?' he said, with a wave of his hand at the old steel and concrete building. Blotches in the walls marked where windows used to be; the concrete blocks used to fill the openings didn't quite match the rest of the structure. A big truck was backed up to the loading-dock, and another just as large waited in the street, its motor idling at a deafening level. The building was surrounded by a high wire fence, and a guard stood at the gate. There was a hint of military training about his posture; he recognised the car and passed them in with a wave of the hand.

Brett negotiated the narrow lane past the loading-dock with care and parked in a tiny car park. There was room for three other cars.

'A parking space is one of the perks of top management,' he said, seeing her expression. 'We employ more than four people, I'm sure you'll be happy to know.'

'I wouldn't have been surprised. How do your employees get to work?'

'Mostly by bus.'

'Fultonsville doesn't have any public transport.'

'And you think they'll be disappointed? Don't bet on it. The ones who do drive to work have to walk twelve blocks from the nearest car park.'

'In Fultonsville,' she said thoughtfully, 'there is scarcely anything that's farther than twelve blocks away.'

'That's an exaggeration, and you know it. If I had said anything of the kind, you would have jumped straight down my throat.'

She smiled, unwillingly. 'Probably. I'd like to talk to some of your employees.'

'Feel free.'

'I'm going to ask them how they feel about the move,' she warned.

'Don't you think I've already asked? We have some who don't want to leave the city, of course. Many of those people are employees who have been with us for years, and for them we're working out early-retirement packages so that they don't lose by our decision. But the younger ones—the ones who have been with the company for ten or twenty years—are anxious to move.'

'I got the impression that the decision to move was yours. And yet you say "we" and "our," as if you have to consult others.'

'My board of directors makes the decisions, of course.'

'But isn't that a rubber-stamp, Brett? Just a blind support of whatever you want to do?'

'It may be that way in other organisations. But years ago Hilliard included its employees in a profit-sharing plan. It's complicated, but it ends up meaning that every employee owns part of the company. That's what the board of directors is about.'

'I see,' she said slowly. 'So it really is a mutual decision to move?'

'The board makes the final judgement, of course, but we polled the workers first.'

'And you're determined to come to Fultonsville?' It was soft, without emphasis.

Brett looked down at her and grinned. 'You aren't going to catch me out, Rebecca,' he warned. 'Until the City Council has made its decision, I have no comment.'

'Not even off the record?'

'Sorry to disappoint you.'

'You're dealing with other towns too,' she observed.

'That's right.'

'Is Fultonsville your first choice?'

'No comment.'

'Which towns are they?'

'You don't really expect me to tell you that, do you?'

'I can find out, you know.'

'Be my guest.'

'Have you been spending as much time in those towns as in Fultonsville?'

'What do you have, a calculator for a brain? I suppose you're going to take the number of hours in a week and figure out how far I could have travelled in that time.'

'It might work.'

'When you're doing your calculations, don't forget about aeroplanes,' he recommended. He stopped at the door of the factory and looked down at her. 'You know, I do like you, Rebecca.'

It made her uncomfortable. The words were innocuous, but the expression in his eyes—the warmth and the dark glint of humour—made her uneasy.

'You aren't supposed to like a person who is doing an investigative report on you,' she said sternly.

He smiled. 'Then I guess you're just going to have to try harder,' he said softly.

They spent the afternoon in the factory. The building

which from the outside looked so old and dingy was brilliantly lighted and hospital-clean inside. It was stainless-steel-lined, it seemed to Rebecca, and full of computerised equipment. The manufacturing lines wound in a complicated pattern over three levels.

'It looks like a maze,' she said, looking up through the machinery.

'It is. That's why we need more space. And don't tell me to start parking my car elsewhere so that I can put an addition on here—that wouldn't even take care of the new research laboratory space we need.'

'But you have labs.' They were standing in the doorway of one as she spoke. 'It's little, but——'

'You can say that again.' A young man in a white laboratory coat looked up from a microscope. 'We're trying to do research in the same lab where we test the finished products to be sure they meet federal standards. It's impossible, so I end up taking work home, and then my wife is furious because I'm making a mess in her kitchen.'

'Rebecca, this is my bacteriologist, Tom Williams. Tom, Rebecca Barclay—sometimes known as Rebel, for reasons that will become apparent when you get to know her better.'

The young man looked vaguely interested. He was near-sighted, and the powerful lenses of his glasses magnified his eyes as he studied Rebecca. 'Glad to meet you. Are you bringing Rebecca to dinner tonight, Brett?'

'Would I miss a chance to eat Peggy's cooking? You'll love it, Rebecca.'

'Oh, I couldn't barge in——' she said.

Tom shook his head. 'The invitation was issued for two.'

'Your friends know you very well,' Rebecca muttered to Brett, under her breath.

'It will give you a chance to talk to my employees,'

Brett pointed out. 'Peggy worked here, too, till the baby was born.'

'And now she's going nuts at home,' Tom added. 'She'd love to see an adult face.'

And what could she say to that? Rebecca asked herself unhappily. Brett had said something about dinner, and she'd been prepared for that. She had planned to tell him, when he suggested a restaurant, that she wanted to rest and change clothes before the play, and that she would just order from room service. But this—what polite way was there to refuse an invitation like this?

There was none, she knew. I've been set up, she thought.

'I'd be delighted,' she said. Out of the corner of her eye, she saw a momentary flash of satisfaction cross Brett's face. Then, once again, he was perfectly composed, showing her around the laboratory.

I'm being absorbed, she thought. He's doing this for a reason. What is it that Brett Hilliard is trying to hide?

CHAPTER SEVEN

BY the end of the afternoon, Rebecca's head was swimming. With Brett always at her elbow, she had seen the process of chocolate-making from the time the cacao beans entered the building until the finished chocolates were ready for testing and packaging.

She watched as the bits of solid chocolate were extracted from the shells, and then crushed at high temperatures to liquefy the cocoa butter. Then Brett showed her how the liquid was further refined and mixed with other ingredients before it could be used for chocolate-making.

'You must use tons of cacao beans,' she said, finally, raising her voice to be heard over the rumble of a huge mixer that was stolidly chewing through a mass of semi-sweet chocolate.

'Not as many as we'd like. We have to buy a great deal of already-processed chocolate, because——'

'I know,' she said, thoughtfully. 'Not enough room.'

He nodded at her approvingly, as if she was a particularly bright student. 'At the new plant, we'll be doing all our own roasting, to protect the quality of our product. We'd have no trouble selling the excess—we've already done the market surveys.'

When the tour ended in the packaging department. Brett and Tom Williams both watched appreciatively as she tried to sample each variety. Rebecca finally admitted defeat, giving up before she was half-way through the list.

'You'd soon get tired of those if you worked here,' Tom said.

'Shh, Tom,' Brett chided him. 'The official line is that

no one ever gets tired of Hilliard chocolates. But it's just as well, Rebecca. You wouldn't want to ruin your dinner.'

'The heck with dinner,' she said. 'This is a chocolate-lover's dream—to be let loose in this place and told to try anything I like!'

Brett laughed. 'Nevertheless, I think it's time you stopped. Let's go back to my office.'

'I haven't had a chance to talk to any of your workers——'

'Tomorrow,' he said. 'You can wander around to-morrow all you like.'

'I was beginning to think you'd never let me out of your sight,' she said tartly.

He looked down at her with a smile. 'I think I could be forgiven for being cautious,' he said. 'You do own stock in the competition. Perhaps you're a spy.'

'Three shares hardly counts.'

'That's true. But how do I know it's only three shares? You told me that, but perhaps it's really three hundred. Or three thousand.'

'Why stop there? Why not conclude that I own the whole company, and I've been planted in Fultonsville for the last four years, just digging myself in and waiting for you to make your move so that I could sabotage you?'

'It's conceivable,' he conceded. 'Your job would be good cover.'

She groaned. The man was impossible!

Outside the door of his office, in what was really no more than a bend in the hallway, was a small desk with a clean surface and a hooded typewriter. Rebecca studied it and remembered the woman who had so firmly refused to give her Brett's home telephone number.

'Isn't your secretary here today?' she asked politely.

'Nope. Said she wasn't feeling well.'

'I'll bet,' Rebecca said under her breath. She's probably sulking at home, she thought, jealous because

someone else is getting all the attention. As if I want
Brett's attention! I wish he'd just leave me alone——

'Why did you do this?' she asked abruptly.

His eybrows rose.

'Oh, don't pretend you don't know what I'm talking
about,' she said. 'You arranged this trip. You planned it,
and talked the station manager into going along with it. I
want to know why it was so important to you that I come
up here.'

'Because,' he said, levelly, 'I thought you might benefit
from seeing both sides of a story.'

It wasn't true—or at least it wasn't the whole truth, she
amended. She knew in the pit of her stomach that he was
lying. But right now she couldn't force him to tell the
truth, so there was nothing more she could do. She
sighed, and thought, you should have had more sense
than to push the matter. He might have given himself
away, if you hadn't shown your hand.

'Besides,' he added, 'it was a way to see you again
without Paul interfering.'

She tried to laugh about it, but his words had left her
breathless. I would like it to be true, she thought. A
twinge of fear swept over her, a shivery reminder of what
she had felt at lunch. Am I going crazy? she wondered.

His office was a tiny windowless room at the back of
the building, on the top floor. 'Not exactly the executive
suite,' she said. 'I'll bet your new office will be plush.'

'That's right,' he agreed cheerfully. 'It's going to have
room for an extra chair, at least.'

He tossed a roll of paper on his desk. 'There are the
blueprints for the new plant,' he said. 'And here is a set of
drawings, to the same scale, for this building. I thought
you might like to compare them.'

She unrolled the drawings idly. The details of the
blueprints meant nothing much to her; she hadn't been
trained to read them. But she did know psychology, and
business, and she knew that businesses didn't invest

money in architects' fees unless they were very serious indeed.

'What you're really saying,' she observed, 'is that you're going to build a plant in Fultonsville no matter what sort of deal the City Council offers you.'

'What makes you say that?'

'These.' She tapped a manicured fingernail on the roll of paper. 'You wouldn't have gone to so much trouble and expense——'

'Those, my dear, are preliminary plans, quite adaptable for use in any of the cities we're considering. And for your information, yes, I have walked the sites in those other towns, with architects and surveyors, and talked about the special requirements of building there.'

'Oh.' She felt deflated.

He leaned back in his chair and studied her. 'For your private information, Rebecca——'

She shook her head. 'Nothing off the record.'

'All right, dammit, then put it on the air if you like. Fultonsville started out as our second choice. Does that make you any happier?'

She turned the statement over in her mind, and struck. 'But now it isn't second choice—that's what you're implying.'

'Perhaps.'

'What changed your mind, Brett? What made it number one?'

'Why are you so certain it didn't go down to number three?'

'Because I'm sitting here, and reporters from those other towns aren't.'

He grinned. 'I believe in giving personal attention to the press.'

'I can see that,' she said tartly. 'You didn't answer my question, so I will. You'll get a better deal from Fultonsville than anywhere else—that's what it is, isn't it?'

'Something like that,' he conceded. 'What made you choose that particular radio station. Isn't it because you could get the best deal there?'

'I'm not being paid with public money.'

'And I am tired of arguing about it with you. It's futile to try to reason with someone whose mind is closed. Come on, Tom and Peg are expecting us for dinner. I hope you'll make an attempt to be civil to them, no matter how you feel about me.'

He stood up abruptly, ending the conversation.

The drive from the factory to the Williamses' apartment was silent. They didn't speak for long minutes. Rebecca hadn't known that a car—even a luxury car—could be so quiet.

She was thinking about his words. There had been something final in the way he had said that her mind was closed. It wasn't true—or was it?

Would Brett be doing anything so terrible, if the City Council offered that deal and he accepted it? He hadn't sought it out, or blackmailed them into improving the offer, she was sure of that. If there had been anything of that sort, there would have been rumours all over town; it would have been impossible to keep such a thing quiet.

And he did have an obligation to his employees, to run the business at a profit. It didn't take a management genius to see that there were problems here—too little space, too much equipment crammed in. It couldn't be an efficient plant when people had to walk around each other to work. And there was no way to make it larger, here. He really had no choice about making a move.

And, if he had to move his business, why shouldn't he look for the best location—the one that offered him the greatest chance of making a profit?

You're making excuses for him, she told herself. You're finding all kinds of reasons for him to act the way he does, and you're violating the reporter's code that has been your law for so many years. You're letting personalities come into business, and it's time to ask a few tough questions of yourself, Rebecca Barclay.

It wasn't the first time she had dealt with a charming man in this business, she reflected. But it was the first time she had allowed herself to fall in love with one——

The thought had come so naturally that it took an instant to register. When the full weight of it struck her, she stopped breathing with the shock of it.

It can't be, she told herself blankly. It simply cannot have happened. He's a charming scoundrel, and he's right that I haven't been quite fair, quite open-minded. Perhaps I've known all along, in the back of my mind, that I wasn't quite safe around him, and so I've been less than fair. But it's been no more than that. I can't be in love with Brett Hilliard; I'm engaged to be married——

And about time you remembered it, too, she told herself grimly. It was the first time the thought of Paul had crossed her mind in hours.

'You're right,' she said abruptly. 'I did make up my mind and then refuse to hear anything to the contrary. And I'd like to talk about it.'

He didn't say anything, and at first she wondered if he had been so deeply buried in his own thoughts that he hadn't even heard. But a moment later he parked the car in a paved space beside a huge apartment complex, turned the engine off, swivelled to face her, and sat for a long moment looking into her eyes. Then he said, 'Welcome back to the real world, Rebecca,' and smiled.

It made her just a little dizzy. She wondered, with a tiny tingle of fear in her veins, what she had started.

Peggy Williams was a small, slim blonde who looked scarcely old enough to be the mother of the year-old child she held. She paused only to hand the tired little boy to Tom and to give Brett a quick hug, and then she drew Rebecca into the kitchen.

'Sorry to drag you off like this,' she said, 'but I have to

keep an eye on dinner, and if you and Brett are going to
make it to the theatre on time, I'd better start the steaks.'

The kitchen was tiny and the counter tops were piled
with stacks of dishes, pans, and bowls. 'Sorry about the
mess,' Peggy said. 'There are days when I'd trade the
baby for a dishwasher without a second thought.'

'May I help?'

'No need. I'll clean it up after dinner.'

'But I might as well be useful now.' Rebecca started to
run hot water.

'I certainly didn't bring you out here to wash dishes,
but I'm not foolish enough to argue with you about it,'
Peggy said with a smile. 'Here's an apron. I'll be so glad
when we get settled into a new house——'

'In Fultonsville,' Rebecca said, without emphasis.

Peggy nodded. 'Tom and I drove down a couple of
weeks ago and looked around. Nothing official, of
course—we can't even talk to the real estate people yet.'

'But the decision has been made.' She should have felt
triumphant, because Peggy had confirmed what she had
suspected all along—that Brett's mind had been made up
already, and that he was simply waiting to see whether
the City Council would better the deal. But she didn't. In
fact, she thought, a little confused, she felt almost glad
that Hilliard Confectioners would be coming to Fultonsville, no matter what.

'I certainly hope it's Fultonsville,' Peggy said. 'If I was
positive that's where we're going, I'd have said the heck
with diplomacy and gone to look at houses. There was
one I fell in love with on sight, and I wanted to see the
inside so much——' She looked around the kitchen with
distaste, and pushed a pan of steaks under the broiler.
'We've lived here for two years, and I think it's been
worse the last few weeks, when we know we'll be moving
somewhere else.'

'You haven't thought about buying a house here?'

'It's a two-edged sword, you see. Property is so

expensive in this city that with Tom's salary alone, we can't quite manage it. I used to work at Hilliard, too, and with me working we could afford to buy. But that means I'd have to leave the baby in day-care, and——'

'You don't want to do that.'

'It isn't that I wouldn't. I mean, I don't have any deep-seated notions about how he'll be scarred for life if his mother works. But I can't find a day-care centre that I really trust. Besides, if Tom and I are both working and commuting to the factory from the suburbs, when would we have time to enjoy our house?'

'I see what you mean. You're caught in a trap, aren't you?'

'Some of the people at the factory drive an hour or more to get to work. That's not my kind of life.'

Rebecca shook her head. She was thinking about how, in Fultonsville, she could walk to the radio station in all but the worst weather. 'Can I quote you?' she asked. 'You know I'm a reporter——'

Peggy smiled. 'I know that's what Brett says,' she agreed.

'What does that mean?'

'You really are one? I'll be darned. Brett doesn't like reporters, you know.'

'What does he have to hide?' Rebecca asked thoughtfully.

Peggy turned the steaks over and put them back under the broiler. 'That sounded cynical,' she observed. 'He doesn't have anything to hide, exactly; he just prefers not to talk about himself.'

Rebecca considered that as she finished washing the stack of dishes. What did any of them really know about Brett Hilliard? she thought. Beyond his job, and his personal charm—did she really have any idea what made the man tick?

'He has to deal with reporters, of course, for the company's sake. But when it comes to personal things,

Brett is a very private person,' Peggy went on. 'He's not
like his grandfather. That guy wanted his name on
everything he did. That's why there's a Hilliard wing at
one of the hospitals, and a Hilliard fund at the Art
Institute——'

Rebecca said thoughtfully, 'That explains why the
woman at the museum restaurant knew Brett.'

'He took you there? I'm amazed; he usally stays a mile
from the place, on general principles. I think he wants to
avoid taking credit for what his grandfather did.' Peggy
took a bowl of potato salad and a plate of sliced tomatoes
from the refrigerator. 'It's an awfully simple menu
tonight,' she said. 'And we're eating out on the patio—
it's the only place that ever gets a breath of cool air. I
hope you don't mind.'

'Mind? I'm touched that you invited me to come.'

'Well, Brett's pretty special to us. So whenever he——'
Peggy broke off and hurried to remove the steaks,
leaving Rebecca to speculate about the end of the
sentence.

Whenever Brett asked a favour? Whenever Brett
wanted help? Whenever Brett had a tiresome person to
entertain.

It doesn't matter, she told herself. I'm here to do a job,
and personal feelings don't enter into it.

When they took the food out to the patio, the men were
discussing employee morale. 'Everybody's restless,
Brett,' Tom was saying. 'The uncertainty is driving us all
crazy.'

'Another week or two at most and we'll know,' said
Brett. He looked up at Rebecca with a smile and made
room for her beside him on the porch swing. 'I don't
suppose it would do me any good to ask you not to repeat
that, Rebecca.'

She shrugged. 'I thought everybody already knew it.'

Peggy unfolded a napkin from the basket of hot rolls.
'It isn't only the uncertainty that's making us all nervous,'

she said. 'It's the heat this summer, and the feeling that
you're never quite safe here. We've had three burglaries
in this building in the last year. I want to get out of the
city, Brett; I don't want my kids to go to school here.'

He laughed. 'Peg, I said you have to wait another week
or two for a decision, not four years. Cultivate patience,
my dear. It's a virtue.'

'Yes, but it will be a year or more before the factory's in
operation.'

'Don't bet on it.'

'You can do it faster than that?' Rebecca turned to
him. 'How?'

'The only way you'll find out is if the City Council gets
down to business soon.' He laughed at the expression on
her face, and ruffled her hair with a casual hand.
'Otherwise, it will remain my professional secret.'

'I can find out,' she said.

'Curiosity, my dear, is not only your stock in trade, but
it may be your fatal flaw.'

She settled herself with a little flounce, and saw out of
the corner of her eye the meaningful look that Peggy and
Tom had exchanged. Then, abruptly, she understood
what Peggy had meant. *Brett's pretty special to us*, she had
said.

They both think this is a romance, Rebecca thought.
They think that it can't be business, or Brett wouldn't be
spending all this time with me . . .

She reconstructed the logic that Tom and Peggy must
have followed: Fact one, Brett dates a lot of women. Fact
two, I'm not half bad-looking. Fact three, he doesn't like
reporters. Conclusion: he must see more in me than my
profession.

It was enough to take her breath away, and it took a
few minutes to talk herself out of it. That's nonsense, she
told herself firmly. I'm wearing a diamond ring. I'm
obviously not in the market for a man. How can any sane

person think I'd be romantically interested in Brett Hilliard?

The answer was abrupt and unexpected: because any normal woman would be.

She stole a look up at him under her long dark lashes. Relaxed, with a glass of wine in his hand, surrounded by his friends, he was a different man from the one she had met before. She had known, of course, that he possessed charm; he had used it on her. But tonight there was no plan, no conscious effort to charm. It was automatic on his part. He simply oozed charisma, and despite her efforts to stay aloof, she could feel it soaking into her bones, like the heat from a tub of steaming bubbles.

And this, she thought, was only the casual charm of the man. What kind of magnetic field could he produce if he really was attracted to a woman? No wonder, she thought, that he didn't seem to have a shortage of feminine attention. What would it be like, she speculated, if Tom and Peggy had been right—if Brett's interest in her was more than professional? What if those gorgeous clear brown eyes were to look deep into hers, and what if he were to say, 'Rebecca——' with the slightest husky catch in that beautiful voice, as if she meant the world to him?

You, she told herself sternly, are crazy even to think about it. Yes, he's a handsome man. And you are engaged to the man you love, and you've got no business speculating about anyone else. What was it Brett himself had said a few minutes ago, about curiosity being her fatal flaw? Well, he was right, and if she didn't get herself under control, she was going to cause herself a whole lot of trouble.

'Rebecca,' a husky voice murmured in her ear, and she jumped, her heart rocking perilously. Surely this was just a fragment of that stupid daydream——

But Brett's head was bent close to hers, his breath tickling her ear.

She sat up straight, primly, half aware of the grin that Tom was doing his best to smother.

'You seem to have gone away for a while,' that smooth voice went on. His hand had slipped to the nape of her neck, under the curtain of auburn hair. 'Tom was asking you why you chose radio as a career. You didn't seem to hear him, my dear.'

'Certainly I heard,' she said, coolly. She wished he would take his hand off her neck; his probing fingers were making her uncomfortably warm. 'I was just thinking about my answer.'

'Of course,' said Brett soothingly.

'You're right about curiosity being part of it,' she said, and looked up at him, intending to treat this like the casual event it was. But he was so close, and his hand resting against her skin felt like a red-hot brand. 'I like learning about new things,' she said, hardly knowing what she was saying. 'I like asking questions, and I don't mind if sometimes they're dumb questions and I end up looking like a fool. I think that's part of what my listeners like about the show—it's very human, and they might have asked the same things.'

'Why not television?' Tom asked. 'You've certainly got the looks for it.'

She shook her head. 'It's sweet of you to say that, but I haven't really. I'm too fair-skinned—I wash out under the television lights, and I look pale and sick, and my freckles are about the size of dimes——'

Brett's finger brushed her cheekbone, gently. 'I like your freckles,' he said.

'I know you do,' Rebecca said. 'But you don't have to wear them, so your opinion doesn't count.'

He laughed, and moved just a little away from her. It made her feel more comfortable, but at the same time just a little lonely.

Her relief was short-lived, though, because only moments later Brett glanced at his wristwatch and said,

'We've got to be going, Rebecca, if we're going to be on time for the curtain.'

Tom and Peggy didn't press them to stay. They're probably anxious to have us gone so that they can discuss us Rebecca thought, with a flicker of amusement, Too bad that they have such a very wrong idea! They weren't the first young couple she had run into who, once they had discovered the bliss of marriage for themselves, seemed determined to pair off the rest of the world.

'I hope I'll see you again,' she told them at the door.

Peggy gave her a conspiratorial smile. 'Perhaps we'll be in Fultonsville.'

'There's a jazz festival next week down on the riverbank,' Rebecca said. 'We have one every summer— it's a big event for the town. You should come down and see what you think of it.'

'That's a good idea. Brett, do you think you'll have made up your mind by then?'

'Why does everyone seem to think this is entirely my decision?' he complained.

'Because it is,' Rebecca told him. 'And everyone but you seems to know it.'

The theatre was an old one, once used for vaudeville shows and recently restored to all its former grandeur. It was in the heart of the Loop, and driving there from the suburban outskirts took them through a variety of neighbourhoods and on to one of the busiest freeways in the world.

'I didn't realise it was so far,' Rebecca said finally.

'The sheer size of the city complicates a lot of things. Take cacao beans, for instance——'

'Must I?' Rebecca asked.

He smiled. 'Have I worn out the topic? I was just going to say that if they come in by barge through Lake Michigan, they have to be off-loaded and carted across the city. But if you're tired of the subject——'

'Not tired of it, exactly. But it isn't working hours——'

'Does that mean you don't want to talk about chocolates during the interval?'

'Something like that.'

'You've got it. I won't breathe a word about business till tomorrow morning. Tonight, let's have fun.'

That wasn't exactly what I meant either, she thought. But after all, what harm could there be in having an evening of fun?

The evening was frosted with enchantment, she thought dreamily as they came out of the theatre. The play had been as wonderful as Brett had promised; Rebecca had laughed till her sides ached, and then, as the tone of the play changed in the twist of an instant, had been ready to shed tender tears.

Brett had seemed to share her moods. She had been a little afraid that, because he had seen the play before, he might be bored by it. But they seemed to find hilarity in the same things, and during one of the tender moments, he had reached for her hand, and held it till the end of the act.

During the interval, they had been greeted in the theatre lobby by half a dozen people; some of them had looked at Rebecca with warmth, others with a distant coolness, but all had been obviously curious. Brett had not satisfied their inquisitiveness by explaining who she was; he had merely returned their greetings, introduced them to 'my friend, Rebecca', and moved on, his hand warmly possessive on the small of her back. It had left her feeling protected and pampered and very, very important.

'It's a nice night,' he said as they came out on to the street after the last curtain call. 'Shall we walk over to your hotel?'

She nodded, insanely glad that the evening would go on just a little longer, and he took her hand.

'We can walk down State Street,' he said, 'and window-shop, if you like.'

The stream of people coming from the theatre was soon left behind, but the streets of the city were never quiet. Tonight, however, it seemed as if they were surrounded by a bubble, Rebecca thought—a protective envelope that shut out the world.

It was silly, she thought, but true nonetheless that sharing laughter drew two people closer together. It was especially true when they discovered that the same sort of things made them laugh. Paul would have liked the play, but he wouldn't have loved it as she had. While Brett— she felt a sudden stab of disloyalty that she even dared to compare the two of them.

The windows of the big department stores on State Street were brilliantly lighted. After the darkness of the theatre, the light made Rebecca feel as if she was on public display.

She brushed an experimental finger across her eyelid. 'I laughed so hard that I cried,' she said, 'and now I feel as if my mascara is running down my cheeks.'

Brett stopped and turned her gently to face him. He looked down into her face as if he had never seen her before, and the inspection made her nervous. It was a long moment before he said, with a husky catch in his voice, 'If this is what you look like when you've been crying, you should do it more often. You're beautiful.'

She swallowed hard, and decided that the safest way to handle that was to ignore it. She didn't want him to say things like that to her. Too many times, men had tried to buy her co-operation on stories by paying her compliments. She didn't want Brett to be like that. It would have been different, perhaps, if he had meant it, but— that's out of the question, Rebecca, she told herself firmly. Of course he didn't mean it.

And that, for some obscure reason, made her feel like crying all over again.

She started walking again, and when he caught up with her and tried to take her hand, she resisted.

'What did I say that was so terrible?' he asked. 'It's true. Does it upset you, to know that I find you very attractive?'

His voice was husky, but there was a hard edge to it that frightened her, made her doubt her own sanity. She looked up at him with confusion in her eyes. 'I think I'd better go straight to the hotel.'

'If you wish,' he said. They didn't speak again, and he didn't try to hold her hand, as they walked the few blocks to the hotel. When she would have said goodbye in the lobby, he shook his head. 'I'll see you to your room,' he said, and she knew from the tone of his voice that there was no use arguing with him about it.

And, if she admitted the truth, she wasn't entirely reluctant to have him come up with her. It had been such a perfect evening, until those last few moments. She didn't want to say goodnight to him in a public lobby. She didn't want to say goodnight to him at all . . .

She unlocked her door and turned to tell him how much she had enjoyed the evening. His fingers cupped her face and turned it up to him. He had moved very close to her, and his eyes were dark and intense.

She looked up at him, and froze. 'No,' she said, but her voice was uncertain and quavering.

'Why not? Is it so awful of me to want to kiss you goodnight?'

He was standing in such a way that he blocked any escape she might have tried to make. She could scream, of course, she told herself, but what would that accomplish? The manager no doubt knew Brett—everyone in Chicago, it was beginning to seem to her, knew Brett—and the only thing she would succeed in doing would be to get herself kicked out of the hotel altogether.

Besides, she admitted wearily, God help me, it's true. I

have fallen in love with him. And I want to know what it would be like to have him kiss me, not in that teasing way of his, but a real kiss——

The memory of one swift embrace, in the greenhouse the night of her father's barbecue, rose to haunt her. It had been the briefest of kisses, and yet there was something that made her want to know——

He seemed to read the traitorous wish in her eyes, and he reached over her shoulder and pushed the door open. She knew she should protest, but before she could find words, the door had clicked shut behind them and she was in his arms.

Just a goodnight kiss, she told herself. It's nothing more than that. The man spent a lot of money and time on you tonight, and if he wants a kiss in return, it isn't going to hurt you. It's nothing to feel ashamed of, or guilty about——

She was lying to herself, and she knew it the instant that his lips brushed hers. The brief moment in the greenhouse hadn't been accidental; the cloud of charm that surrounded him was almost like an anaesthetic, disconnecting all her inhibitions, making her forget everything except him.

She didn't hear the tiny moan she uttered; she was too lost in the sensations created as his hands moved gently over the soft fabric of her dress, sending exquisite arrows of flame through every cell. But Brett heard, and something primitive flared in him. He pulled her even closer, as if he was trying to absorb her body into his, and took her mouth again, more harshly this time.

And suddenly she knew that this was where she belonged, where she wanted to spend the rest of her days. Everything else was forgotten—Paul, Gwen, the story she had come to Chicago to explore. The only thing worthy of exploration now was Brett himself, and the shocking but undeniable truth that had come to her— that in the midst of fighting him, she had somehow come to love him as well.

'I want you, Rebecca,' he whispered, 'so much——'

She raised her eyes to his, knowing that her longing was written there in the language all lovers know. He drew a sharp, rasping breath, as if he could not trust what he saw, and then he was kissing her again, his mouth drawing lines of fire that promised to scorch her soul.

He undressed her slowly, like a doll—too slowly for her to bear, and the touch of his fingers against her silky skin brought shudders of desire rushing through her body, making her ache for his possession, for an answer to the questions that haunted her. There was no hesitation left in her, no nagging doubt, just the knowledge that this was something beyond her control, something she had to do if she was ever to know peace again.

He made her wait until the sultry colour of her eyes told him that all her fears were gone. His patience seemed inexhaustible, until the end, when his control too seemed to shatter and they tumbled together off the edge of the world, into a warm and dark abyss that somehow wasn't frightening at all, as long as they were together . . .

There was no time to recover, no time to think about what had happened to them. On the bedside table, the telephone rang. The shrill buzz jolted along Rebecca's nerves like an electric shock, and she jerked away from him. There was only one person who could be calling; one person who knew in which hotel she would be staying.

Oh, my God, she thought, still dizzy with the passion Brett had so thoroughly aroused. It's Paul. I'm still engaged to him, and I'm in bed with another man. I have to straighten this out——

Brett pulled her back against his chest. 'Let it ring,' he whispered.

She shook her head and fought to be free of him. She grabbed for the telephone as if it was some sort of life preserver.

'Rebecca,' Paul said. 'I've been trying to get you for hours.'

'I'm sorry, Paul. I just came in—we worked late, you see, and——'

Brett grinned. He sat up beside her, his hands at her waist, and began to nibble gently at her earlobe.

Rebecca tried to brush him away as if he was an insect, and he retaliated by sliding his hands up till he cupped her breasts, pinning her spine against his chest.

The involuntary breath she drew only pressed her breasts more firmly into his palms, and Rebecca couldn't prevent herself from uttering a breathless little cry at the sensation.

Paul heard it. 'What's going on, Rebecca?'

'Nothing——'

'Now that hurts my feelings,' Brett breathed into her ear.

'Paul, I——' I can't tell him, she thought. Not with Brett here, listening, enjoying every word. Not until I've sorted things out for myself——She swallowed hard. 'Can I call you tomorrow?'

'Rebecca, I did not waste my money calling you so I could just say hello and goodnight. I have some important——'

'Paul, I'm awfully tired.' She was panicky; Brett was still holding her hard against his chest, and he had started to plant kisses along the nape of her neck. Her throat was tight; she was afraid that her voice would crack. 'I'll talk to you tomorrow.' She put the telephone down on his protest.

'Good girl,' Brett whispered. His hands tightened, pulling her off balance and down beside him, snuggling her against the broad warmth of his chest. 'And now a little more time for us——'

'Please, just leave me alone.' Her voice was shaky, but it was the best she could do.

He raised himself on one elbow and looked down at

her. 'Something tells me I'm going to have a score to
settle with Paul,' he said conversationally.

'Doesn't it bother you that I'm engaged to marry him?'

'Not in the least. Should it?'

'Just go away,' she whispered. 'I have to think——'

'Why don't you stop thinking, which will only get you
into trouble.' His hands wandered down across the curve
of her hip, bringing a gasp. 'And let's make love again.'

'No, please, Brett!'

His hands stilled, warm against the sensitive skin. She
took advantage of the moment to twist away from him
and buried her face in the pillow.

Brett sighed. 'Rebecca, you have the most over-
developed conscience I've ever run into,' he said. 'You're
stubborn enough to deny yourself pleasure just to spite us
both—so I'll do as you ask and go home. You think about
it, in your solitary bed tonight. And when you've decided
what you want, let me know.'

'Just get out of here!'

As he dressed, she huddled under a blanket, afraid to
look at him, yet wanting to watch him and gloat over the
masculine strength of the body that had given her such
pleasure. Her face burned with embarrassment.

'By the way, don't worry about your reputation.' His
voice was curt, clipped. 'I won't tell the pretend banker if
you don't.'

'I have no intention of telling Paul anything,' she said
icily. From the corner of her eye, she watched as he
slipped his tie under his collar, leaving the ends dangling.
She wanted to reach up and take hold of it, and pull him
back to her . . .

'Then we neither of us have a thing to worry about,' he
said comfortably. 'I'll see you in the morning, Rebecca. I
hope you sleep well, but if you don't, and you decide
you'd like some company . . .'

'I won't!'

He paused at the door. 'I'd be delighted to keep you

from being lonely. Just call. I can be here in ten minutes, and I guarantee you won't have time to worry about Paul.'

He didn't need to be so crass, she fumed, and struck back blindly, determined to hurt him. 'I suppose you did that so if I write a story you don't like, you can destroy me!'

There was a long, cold silence. She peeped at him through her lashes, and was frightened by the hardness in his face. Then the door closed quietly behind him, and Rebecca turned over to bury her face in the pillow again. Her skin was clammy now where he had touched her, chilled with the sweat of their passion and the sudden loss of his comfortable warmth. Her body ached for his caresses, and she almost cried out for him to come back.

My God, she thought. What is happening to me? And what am I going to tell Paul?

CHAPTER EIGHT

'THIS is the only job I've ever had,' the old man said. His hands didn't stop moving as he talked. Not a motion was wasted as he worked his way through a tray of cherry nougat centres, coating each with thick, rich chocolate. 'Been dipping chocolates for Hilliard's since I was a boy.' He glanced across the table to where his apprentice was working, at a much slower pace, and shook his head. 'You'll have to pick your speed up,' he told the young man gently. 'There's a rhythm to it.'

Rebecca, who had just finished a brief on-the-job training session herself, felt nothing but compassion for the apprentice. The job certainly wasn't as easy as the old man made it look.

She glanced at her tape recorder to be certain it had caught that last remark, and licked a smear of chocolate off her index finger.

'Yep,' the old man said. 'This Mr Hilliard's grandfather hired me when I was fifteen. I've been with the company ever since. Those were the days when everything we sold was hand-dipped.' He sounded wistful. 'Then labour got to be too expensive and the machines came in. Now only a few of our chocolates are hand-dipped.'

'What will you do when the new factory opens?'

'I'll be there.'

'But——' She paused, embarrassed.

'But I'm too old to move, is that what you were going to say?' His eyes twinkled gently. His hands didn't miss a motion. 'Doesn't matter. As long as my fingers hold out, I'll be dipping. What else is there to do?'

'Do you really mean that you'd move to Fultonsville?'

'Or anywhere else. I'll take Mr Hilliard's word for it

127

that it's a nice place. Besides, he asked me to come. He wants to hire a few new apprentices—have me teach them how to do it, so we can expand the hand-dipped line again.'

'That,' said Brett's mellow voice behind them, 'is not supposed to be publicly announced.'

The old man grinned. 'Your lady won't spoil things for you, Mr Hilliard.'

'I wish I was as certain as you are,' Brett murmured. 'Have you had fun all day, talking to my employees, Rebecca?' There was a faintly cynical twist to his voice.

She checked her tape again and shut the recorder off. 'I've had a fascinating time.' She had scarcely seen Brett all day; he had picked her up at the hotel that morning, driven her out to the factory—keeping up a steady stream of gently non-committal conversation, which, she thought, was even worse than silence would have been— and left her on the manufacturing floor while he retreated to his office.

His actions had hurt her deeply and left her feeling irritated with herself. She had been just as much to blame for what had happened last night, and they had both said some things that had been meant to hurt. But she hadn't expected that he would simply pretend nothing had happened!

She had spent the day looking over her shoulder to see if Brett was within sight. She hadn't really believed that the cruel words they had exchanged the night before would be the end of it. Surely, harsh words could not destroy the passion they had shared.

She tried to tell herself that it was just as well. The whole thing had been a mistake, that was certain, and the sooner it was forgotten the better. What good could it do to thrash it all out? Better to let it vanish into the realm of unpleasant memory. She threw herself into her work, and tried not to think about the night, even though she wanted to crawl off into a cave somewhere and lick her wounds.

The results of her talks with the employees had been surprising, too. Even the ones who had chosen not to make the move with the company had nothing but praise for Brett Hilliard. Rebecca had heard glowing reports of his efforts to find other work for the people who didn't want to leave the city, and the generosity of the severance pay that they would receive. For a while, her suspicious mind had wondered if everyone who was unhappy with the deal had been told to take the day off. But eventually it began to make sense to her. These people adored Brett Hilliard. They felt overwhelming loyalty to him, and even if the move he was leading them into turned out to be another charge of the light brigade, they would follow him at all costs. It made Rebecca look at him in just a little different light.

Brett drew her aside a little. 'Now that you're done with your work, is it safe for me to come around? Or am I to be accused again of interfering with the freedom of the press?'

She didn't answer, but the faint sarcasm in his voice made her shudder inside. I asked for this, she thought, remembering the last hurtful accusation she had tossed at him.

'I thought I'd better make our dinner reservations early,' he said. 'Friday nights can be a little sticky in this city.'

'Don't feel obliged,' she said. He was standing very close to her, and the sharp tang of his after-shave tickled her nose with longing. Despite her best effort, there was a catch in her voice. She turned away, quickly. 'Thanks for the invitation, but I'm going back to Fultonsville tonight.'

His eyes darkened. 'You were planning to stay over till tomorrow,' he pointed out.

'Surely you don't think I checked out of the hotel this

morning because I was planning to stay with you
tonight!'

'Of course not,' he said politely.

The cool civility made her want to hit him, but she
maintained her outward calm. 'I have my story,' she said
with a shrug. 'I see no reason to stay longer.'

'Did Paul tell you to come home?'

'I haven't talked to him.' Some things, she thought
drearily, have to be done in person.

'I see. You're afraid to stay, so you're running for
cover.'

'What on earth makes you say that?' She didn't give
him a chance to explain. 'I do have reasons for wanting to
get home.'

'Yes, you have to explain things to the pretend banker.
What are you going to tell him, Rebecca? The truth? Or
will you put him off with some story about not feeling
well last night?' His voice was smooth. 'I can't imagine
why he would doubt your loyalty; you would never do
anything to disgrace that diamond ring you wear. Some
girls would, you know. They would think that a trip like
this was an excuse for any sort of behaviour. Some girls
would even climb into bed with the first man who——'

'Stop it! Please, just stop it!'

'Does the truth hurt, Rebecca? You're a liar if you
don't admit that you wanted me last night just as much as
I wanted you.' His voice was low, but there were hard
edges to it that made her shiver. 'And you enjoyed every
instant. If Paul hadn't chosen that particular moment to
call, my dear, we would have made love all night——'

'I don't admit anything of the sort,' she said tightly,
and stepped back quickly as she saw him reach for her.

He smiled, and suddenly the hard planes in his face
seemed to ease. 'I see you're afraid to let me touch you,' he
said softly. 'I must admit, I'd far rather do so in private.
So why don't you stay tonight, Rebecca, and we'll have
dinner and talk about where we go from here. We have a

lot to talk about, you know. Things got a bit out of control last night——'

Out of control, she thought wearily. It was a mild way of describing the earthquake that was threatening to destroy her carefully planned life. I have to get away from him, she thought. I cannot reason things out when I'm near him; all I can do is feel. And I must think——

'No, thanks,' she said crisply. 'The only place I go from here is back to Fultonsville, Brett. On the commuter train, which leaves in two hours.'

'And nothing will change your mind?'

She had never realised that a seduction could be conducted in the middle of a factory assembly line, surrounded by people. Brett wasn't even touching her; only his voice caressed her. 'Nothing will change my mind,' she said, deliberately, and added, as much to convince herself as him, 'I'm going home to my fiancé.'

Brett's eyes went cold, and his voice was hard and mocking. 'By all means, do,' he said. 'You deserve each other. As a gentleman, I have to give in to your wishes. I'll take you to the station.'

'No, thanks,' Rebecca said, with bitterness. 'I'd prefer to call a cab.'

'Oh, I couldn't allow that. You're my guest; I wouldn't want you to be in any danger.'

'I'm in more danger from you than from any dozen muggers!' She bit her lip, instantly sorry for the outburst.

'Perhaps the danger comes from within yourself, Rebecca. That's what you're trying to run away from——'

'I am not running away!'

'Of course not,' he said soothingly. 'Paul should be flattered that you're in such a terrible hurry to get back to him.'

'I don't want you to take me anywhere——' Their disagreement, she saw, was drawing attention from the workers on the assembly line. Rebecca sighed. 'All right,' she said. 'You win.'

'Do I?' he murmured. 'It seemed to me that I was losing rather badly.'

Union Station was packed with travellers leaving the city for the weekend. The concourse was full of hurrying humanity, and the loudspeakers announced the arrival and departure of trains with bewildering frequency.

'Thanks for the ride,' Rebecca said grudgingly as they reached the departure gate. 'I'd have had trouble getting all the way across town in a cab. But you shouldn't have left the car parked like that. You'll get a ticket for certain——'

'I wouldn't want you to have to carry your bag all this way.'

'Brett, it only weighs ten pounds.'

'Do you want to strain your back?'

She gave up. 'All right. Thanks for carrying the bag in. But would you go away now? You can't go out to the train with me, anyway, and nobody's going to kidnap me from the platform——'

'I don't know about that,' he disagreed. 'I'd like to. Despite your stubbornness, I'd like to throw you over my shoulder and drag you back to my apartment and take you to bed, and make you forget Fultonsville and the pretend banker and——'

This, Rebecca told herself, has gone quite far enough. She could feel her knees weakening at the mere memory of last night. She seized on the only way she could find to change the subject. 'The play,' she exclaimed, and her horror was only half-assumed. 'I was going to pay you for my ticket——' She began to rummage in her handbag, and discovered that her wallet had slid clear to the bottom. Damn, she thought. I don't want to stand in the middle of Union Station and take everything out of my bag!

'Ah,' he said. 'You did say you'd pay for it, as a matter

of fact. But since the tickets were a gift from a friend of mine, I couldn't possibly accept cash payment. So I would like to suggest an alternative . . .'

His arms closed about her, resting warmly at her waist, and pulled her close against him. with one hand deep in her handbag, the other holding both the big bag and her travel-bag. Rebecca was helpless to ward off the embrace. She squeezed her eyes shut, hoping that if she couldn't see him, it wouldn't be quite real. But the first demanding touch of his mouth blasted that idea into shreds. This was not make-believe, this was like being turned into a wad of putty, warm and malleable in his bare hands. And last night had not been chance, or accident. The merest brush of his hands was enough to make her shudder with pleasure, as though he really had carried her off to his bed, as he had threatened to do.

It would be so easy, she thought dizzily, to do as he wanted. Every cell, every nerve screamed a protest at the idea of being separated from him.

To an observer, it was the kind of kiss that might have been witnessed on the streets of Fultonsville on any weekend evening. There was nothing about it to embarrass a watching crowd, no wandering hands, no improper caresses. And yet, Rebecca was certain, there was not a person in the concourse who didn't conclude that this was a pair of lovers, about to be separated for weeks or months, or possibly for ever——

'I have to go,' she whispered. 'I can't think like this . . .' It was a plea for understanding.

He sighed. 'I suppose, if you must, you must,' he whispered thickly. 'They just announced boarding for your train.'

Rebecca jerked away from him and turned towards the gate. She was almost sobbing.

He caught up with her a few steps down the platform. 'Rebecca,' he said. 'Don't try to pretend that last night didn't happen. Because it won't go away. You will never be able to forget what we were like together.'

She hardly heard what he had said. She had to get on that train; she wasn't even certain why, any more, but she knew she could not stay in this city for another night. 'I have to talk to Paul,' she said. She was scarcely aware of what she had said.

He swung her around to face him. 'So you're determined to go back to him?' he said. 'Perhaps I should show Paul the technique. I certainly seem to have stumbled on to something that works! But don't pretend, my dear, that you could ever lie in his arms without remembering me——'

'You talk to me like that and dare to call yourself a gentleman!'

'Of course I dare,' he said coldly. 'If I wasn't, I wouldn't have said anything about your train. You had certainly forgotten all about it.' He turned on his heel and strode back towards the station.

She fled down the platform, angry tears blurring her eyes. How dared he talk to her like that, she stormed to herself. How dared he assume that she would willingly give herself to him again? But I would, she admitted painfully.

She turned as she reached her carriage and searched the distant spot of light that was the way into Union Station, but he was gone.

The train attendant offered his arm for support and said, 'Watch your step, miss,' in a gentle tone that held nothing but sympathy.

Oh, my God, Rebecca thought guiltily, even he saw that scene. Had anyone in the world not seen it?

She found a seat by a window in the back corner of the carriage and huddled into it. She watched night fall over the flat land of central Illinois, and saw the moon rise, a thin silver-white streak that seemed to grow larger and more yellow as it rose higher into the sky. She wished on the first brilliant star, a humble wish for guidance. And, by the time the train pulled into Fultonsville station, she knew that whatever else happened, she had to give Paul's ring back. She didn't know what would come after that, whether she would discover that her feeling for Brett was lifelong, or a momentary madness born of purely sexual attraction, but she knew that she could not marry one man while she felt this heart-rending confusion about another.

Paul would understand, she told herself. He simply had to understand.

She called him from the depot. He sounded grumpy when he answered the telephone. 'You said you were going to call me today,' he pointed out. 'I've been waiting around for hours——'

'It's still today,' Rebecca said. 'And I'm home. At least, I'm at the station. Could you come and get me? I don't want to walk ten blocks at night.'

'You're here? In Fultonsville?' His voice had risen with gladness.

Rebecca felt her heart contract. 'Yes. Paul, please come. I need to talk to you.'

'I'll have to throw on some clothes. I'll be there in a few minutes.'

Rebecca chose a bench outside the main door of the station and sat down with relief. It was a pleasant night; the heat of the day had dissipated, leaving a warm breeze that brought the sharp scent of newly cut grass to her nose. She tried to concentrate on the smells, to still the hammering of her heart. This was not going to be easy. She had to be very careful of the words she chose, of the way she broke this to Paul. She might not feel able to marry him, but she still cared about him.

It was nearly twenty minutes before Paul's car pulled up. Rebecca had been getting restless; as soon as the car appeared she hurried towards it.

Before she could say anything, Paul greeted her with an enthusiastic kiss. Guiltily, she remembered the scene

at Union Station; was it possible that Paul might identify
the smell of Brett's after-shave, still clinging to her hair,
to her skin? But he didn't seem to notice anything
unusual.

She tried to will herself to feel the way a woman should
react in the arms of the man she loved. But it was
different. Paul's kisses lacked the power to make her feel
like melted steel, ready to be moulded to a man's
command . . .

'Did you get your story?' he asked. 'I suppose you'll be
at the station all day tomorow putting it together.'

'I wouldn't be surprised. The manager will want it on
the air as soon as possible.' She braced herself for Paul's
protest, and then remembered that it didn't matter any
more. 'Will you come up for coffee? I really need to talk
to you.'

'I can't, honey. I've got to be on the road early in the
morning.'

'On the road?' She was puzzled.

'Yes. You caught me just as I was getting into bed. I
tried to tell you about it last night.'

'Oh.' She swallowed hard.

'Dad had planned to go upstate this weekend to talk to
an important client, but his ulcer kicked up again and the
doctor doesn't want him to go. So he's sending me
instead.' He sounded half frightened, half proud. 'Just
think, Rebecca, in another few months you can go with
me on trips like this.'

It hurt a little, to see his boyish pleasure in the trip and
know that she was going to shatter it. 'Paul, this is really
important. It will just take a few minutes——'

He shook his head. 'I'm really tired, Rebecca. We'll
talk next week, and you can tell me all about your trip.'

As if, she thought, I was a child at show-and-tell!

'You know,' he went on, parking the car beside her
front gate, 'I hope you'll think very seriously while I'm
gone about the radio station. It's going to interfere with

our lives, I'm afraid.' He opened her door and helped her out. 'But we can talk about that on Tuesday when I get home, too. This weekend is a big step for us, honey. If I'm successful, there's no telling what comes next.'

'Paul,' she said, unwilling to let it go on any longer. 'I can't marry you.'

There was a long silence. Paul's forehead knotted, as if he was trying to translate what she had said. 'Rebecca, what on earth has happened to you?'

For one brief instant she contemplated telling him the truth. Then reason and the instinct of self-preservation intervened. In a town the size of Fultonsville gossip wasn't only a habit, it was almost a profession. 'I've been doing a lot of thinking,' she said carefully. 'I just don't think we would suit.'

He started to laugh. 'Oh, Rebecca, don't be foolish! We're from the same stock, the same roots. Of course we'll suit! You're just having an attack of wedding-plan jitters. Every bride does, I'm told.'

Not every bride finds herself in bed with another man, she thought. 'Paul, I mean it.'

He soothed her with a gentle clicking of his tongue. 'You're tired, darling, and let's face it, being around Hilliard for a couple of days is enough to make anyone question anything. I mean, he may be a genius at business, but he's not a comfortable person to be around.'

You can say that again, Rebecca thought wearily.

'That's another reason I wish you'd leave the radio station,' he went on, and patted her hand reassuringly. 'Now you think it over while I'm gone, and we'll talk about it next week. I'm sure by then you'll be ready to laugh about this notion of yours. Mother wants you to come to lunch on Monday, by the way, at the house——'

'Paul, I don't think you're listening.' Her voice was rising. 'I've just told you I don't think we should be engaged any more.'

'Rebecca, I really must ask you to postpone this

discussion until you can talk about it in a reasonable tone of voice. You won't mention anything of the sort to my mother, of course; this sort of nonsense would be very upsetting to her. Now I must get some sleep, dear; I have a long drive tomorrow.' His voice softened as he looked down at her. 'You'll feel better after a good night's sleep.'

Would she? Was she only suffering from wedding jitters? Was there any chance at all that in the morning, free of Brett's disturbing presence, she might regret breaking her engagement? Suddenly Rebecca was so confused that she thought her head might explode.

She turned into Paul's arms, and buried her face in his shoulder. He lifted her chin and kissed her. It was a pleasant enough kiss, an embrace between two people who cared for and respected each other. But she couldn't deny a sense of loss, of longing, when she pulled away from Paul. Why couldn't she feel the same way with him as she did in Brett's arms?

'I'll see you next week,' she said, tremulously.

'We'll get it sorted out then,' he assured her. 'And we'll laugh about it.'

Would they? she wondered. Would the mess her life had become ever be all straightened out again?

'I'm glad that you were able to spare the time to have lunch with me today,' Cleo said.

Rebecca's soup spoon remained poised above her plate for a long moment. Had there been a sarcastic twist to Cleo's words? But the woman's eyes met hers calmly, and Rebecca cursed herself for giving in to an over-active imagination. If there was one thing she hadn't wanted to do today, it was to have lunch with Cleo. And yet, until she and Paul had settled this thing, Rebecca felt that she could hardly refuse. She was still wearing his ring, too. It seemed only polite to make Paul understand that she meant it, before every yokel in town found out that Rebel Barclay wasn't wearing her diamond any more.

'I don't always have time for lunch,' she agreed. 'It was especially nice of you to make it yourself, so we didn't have to hurry at a restaurant.'

'Yes. The food at the club is very good, but I find it gets tiresome.'

And if we don't find something else to talk about, Rebecca thought desperately, I am going to die of terminal triteness!

'I hope that you'll have a few minutes to spare; I'd like to take you through the carriage house. Actually, I wanted you to come for dinner last weekend because I thought it would be nice for you and Paul to see it together, but with first one of you out of town and then the other——'

'Do you mean Paul hasn't seen it yet?' Rebecca knew she shouldn't have broken in, but she couldn't help herself.

'Of course not,' Cleo said with dignity. 'I've had the same decorator for twenty years, and she has always chosen the things for Paul's room. I'm sure he'll be delighted with what she's done in the carriage house.'

Then why bother to show it to him at all? Rebecca thought rebelliously. Why not just move his things in some day when he's at the bank? I'm sure he wouldn't really notice.

Cleo had gone on. 'Calling it the carriage house has been fine all these years, but I think now that we really should come up with a more appropriate name. I believe I'll start referring to it as the guest house. You'll be our very honoured guest, Rebecca.'

Not me, Rebecca thought inelegantly. And I'm glad.

'How are the wedding plans coming along?' Cleo bore on, relentlessly. 'I talked to our pastor yesterday after church, and he happened to mention that you and Paul hadn't been to see him yet.'

After you happened to pointedly ask him, Rebecca thought. 'We may decide to wait a while, Cleo.' Surely, she thought, hinting at the truth was better than telling an outright lie.

'I'm glad to see that you're doing something about those freckles across your nose. I'm sure they'll fade somewhat by winter, but it would be terrible to spoil the effect of a lovely dress with those tomboyish marks.'

Rebecca swallowed hard. I don't have to answer, she thought. It wouldn't do any good, anyway; she would never understand that I don't get freckles on purpose. Some of these are as old as I am——

'I did make a list of the people on Paul's side who must be included in the wedding party.' Cleo pushed a slip of monogrammed stationery across the table.

Rebecca didn't even glance at it. 'Of course, Cleo.' Her tone was pleasant.

Cleo wasn't fooled by the non-committal answer. Her eyes sharpened. 'I really think, my dear, that you should remember this is also Paul's wedding, and he has a right to expect a certain standard.'

Rebecca gave her points for that one. How very much, she thought dreamily, I would like to tell her to go jump off a bluff into the river.

Cleo rose to take the soup bowls back to the kitchen. When she returned with their main course, she was again the gracious hostess. 'Did you enjoy your trip into Chicago, Rebecca dear?'

'Yes, but of course I didn't have a lot of time to myself. I was very busy getting my story.' There, she thought, satisfied. That should sidetrack any doubts about whether I was really working.

'I'm sure you'll miss your job a great deal after the wedding. You young girls with your careers—you make the rest of us feel old and useless.' Her tone was condescending. 'A friend of mine said her husband thought he saw you in Chicago.'

Dread clutched at Rebecca. She had recognised no familiar faces from Fultonsville. Where might this unnamed man have seen her? At the art institute? There was nothing embarrassing there; no reason why Brett shouldn't have taken her to lunch. Or perhaps it had been at the theatre? It had been dark; surely no one could have seen her in the few moments that Brett had held her hand. At the hotel? Her heart was starting to pound a little. She said, trying to keep her voice steady, 'I don't recall seeing anyone I knew——'

'He was mistaken, of course,' Cleo went on, positively. Rebecca wondered why she was so certain. But she told herself that no matter how curious she was, she wasn't dumb enough to ask.

'He's working there for a few weeks,' Cleo explained. 'He goes up on Monday and rides the commuter train home for the weekend. He thought he saw you at Union Station on Friday evening.'

Rebecca's heart was slamming into her ribs, so hard that she thought Cleo must hear the racket in the quiet dining-room.

'But of course it couldn't have been you,' Cleo said, 'because you didn't come back till Saturday.' She smiled. 'You must have a look-alike in Chicago, Rebecca. What a very curious thing.'

CHAPTER NINE

REBECCA started breathing again, very slowly and tentatively, hoping that the pain in her chest would go away. You're all right, she told herself. The world did not cave in under your feet. As long as Cleo thinks that you didn't come home till Saturday, she won't give another thought to the odd behaviour of a redhead at Union Station on Friday night, and she will have no reason to mention it to any of her friends. You're lucky, Rebecca, she told herself. You're a lucky, lucky girl.

I will never let Brett Hilliard within touching distance of me again, she vowed. That guy is trouble, through and through! He simply didn't understand how a small town worked—that Fultonsville was not like Chicago, where no one cared what his neighbour did.

This would be all the lesson she needed, she thought. This scrape with disaster was close enough; only a fool would risk more. And if she was truly blessed, she told herself, Hilliard Confectioners would go somewhere else, and Fultonsville would settle back into its pattern as a sleepy little river town, and Paul and Cleo and everyone else in town would never need to know what had happened there in the city.

She tried to ignore the little pang in her heart at the thought that she might never see Brett again at all—that her resolution to stay away from him might be unnecessary, because he might never come near her again . . .

'Of course,' Cleo went on smoothly, 'my friend's husband doesn't know you well, just by sight, from seeing you around town. It's not surprising that he might have thought it was you. Isn't that an interesting coincidence?'

She didn't wait for an answer. 'Shall we walk over to the carriage house?'

Rebecca nodded. In the carriage house, there would be things to look at, to talk about. Here, sitting across the table from Cleo, she felt as if a yawning trap waited for her.

Besides, she thought, she had to admit to an overwhelming curiosity to see this place where she might have begun her married life, if Brett Hilliard had never come along.

Cleo stopped her as she started to gather up her table setting. 'Don't fuss with the dishes, dear. I have all afternoon to clean the mess up.' She smiled. 'I enjoy keeping my home clean and nice for my husband to come to when he's tired. Being a wife is all the job I need to keep me feeling worth while.'

And that, Rebecca thought, is the dirtiest dig I've ever heard!

The carriage house was large by any standards, built in the same style and trimmed with the same elaborate gingerbread as the main house. The lower floor had space for three cars, but Cleo's Cadillac was alone there at the moment. At the corner of the building was a tiny entry way, with a narrow stairway winding up to the floor above.

Already I don't like it, Rebecca thought. The stairway was narrow and dark and uninviting. But when she reached the top of the stairs she was forced to admit that she had judged the place too quickly. It had originally been one huge room, with windows on all sides. At one end, the decorator had partitioned off a bedroom and bathroom, and a gleaming new kitchen had been installed along one end wall of the remaining large living-room. The carpet was down, and some of the curtains had been hung. Here and there a piece of furniture sat, some finished, others with swatches of upholstery fabrics draped across an arm.

The colours were a pleasant blend of peach and blue. There was nothing actually wrong with the decorating scheme, Rebecca told herself. But, she thought with a pang, how she would have enjoyed designing this herself!

'I see I have some additional work to do,' Cleo said, picking up a couple of upholstery swatches. 'That's the worst part of redecorating, having to decide all these things at once.' She studied the swatch. 'This one, without question.'

Apparently, Rebecca thought, it did not occur to Cleo that it might be polite to ask the preference of the young woman she expected to live in this apartment.

Rebecca walked across the room and looked down from the window above the kitchen sink. It faced Cleo's kitchen.

We could stand and do dishes and wave at each other, she thought. Cleo must have planned it that way.

Thank God, she thought, that I am escaping all this. I would always have felt like a guest here, and a less-than-welcome one at that. I would never have felt free to move a piece of furniture, or change a rug, or leave a dirty dish in the sink——

And though she still saw a great many good qualities in Paul, she could also see now that he would never have stood up to his mother; he would never have backed Rebecca in a bid for independence. We would have lived here in the guest house till his parents were done with the big house, she thought, and then we would have moved in there.

She smiled and chatted with good humour, and thought that Cleo seemed surprised at her pleasantness. Surprised, and perhaps a little confused, she told herself. It made Rebecca's day; it was a much more pleasant form of revenge than telling Cleo to go to hell. That would not have surprised the woman in the least, she decided.

But I cannot keep this pretence up, she told herself.

The very moment Paul comes home, he has to understand that I'm finished, that it will not work.

The diamond engagement ring felt like a lead weight on her hand. I didn't know, she thought, that a lie could weigh so much. It was comforting, at least, to have that decision made. Now, she thought, if she could only get the rest of her thoughts so neatly organised . . .

The thought of Gwen had come back to haunt her. Her mind had been so occupied with her own fears, her own worries, that for a while she had forgotten her sister, and the nagging suspicion that Gwen, too, might have made a fool of herself over Brett Hilliard.

It's your imagination, Rebecca, she told herself. Surely no man was fool enough to carry on intrigues with two sisters at the same time!

And that, she told herself roundly, is pure foolishness. You have no real idea what Brett is capable of. You only know what you want.

Late that afternoon, after the radio show was over, she drove out to her father's house. Perhaps talking to her sister might help, she thought.

Gwen was lying in a deck chair on the patio. She looked up with a smile. 'Haven't seen you for a while.'

'I took Dad at his word. He didn't seem to want me to call.'

'You ought to know by now that he didn't mean what he said.'

'I suppose so. Do you spend all day, every day, lying on the patio?'

'No. I just happen to be here whenever you stop by. Have a glass of iced tea and tell me what's bothering you, Rebecca.'

Gwen, she realised, looked more relaxed than she had in a week. 'Cleo, for one. But let's not go into it. You're in an awfully good mood today—I'd hate to spoil it.'

'I'm in such a good mood I can't stand myself. Bill's coming next weekend.'

'Oh, really?'

'Yes. It's the first time he's left that business of his since he started it three years ago. We're going to take the kids down the River Road on our way home——'

Rebecca flung her arms around her sister. 'I'm so happy for you,' she said.

'I've been a confused mess, haven't I?'

'Well, yes, now that you mention it. What happened?'

'Since you're going to be married yourself, I'll give you the secret,' Gwen said, with a pompous air that reminded Rebecca of Cleo Fredericks. 'When you love a guy enough, sometimes you just have to call him up and tell him that you can't stand what he's doing but you love him enough to put up with it anyway——'

'Gwen,' Rebecca said tenderly, 'you are giving a bad name to women's liberation.'

'Why? True liberation, my dear, is the freedom to choose how we want to live. Right now, I want to go home and take care of my husband and two kids.'

'I'm proud of you.'

'And if a woman is really lucky,' Gwen went on, with a tiny tremor in her voice, 'when she makes that phone call, her man has been missing her enough to say that he'll listen and he'll change. That's why he's coming out to get us, instead of the kids and me going straight home. It isn't going to be easy, but when you love each other enough——' She looked at Rebecca with concern in her eyes.

'I'll let you in on a secret too,' Rebecca said lightly. 'I'm not going to marry Paul.'

'Glory be!' Gwen gestured towards Rebecca's left hand. 'Don't tell me he was gentleman enough to let you keep the ring.'

'Not exactly. It isn't all settled yet.'

'Becky Barclay, do you mean you haven't told him?'

'I tried,' Rebecca said defensively.

'Well, don't back down.' Gwen was frowning.

'Perhaps there's something I should tell you. I don't deny that when I first got here, I flirted with Brett. I don't know, I might even have had an affair with him, if he had been willing. But he just laughed at me——'

Rebecca's heart started to glow a little. I knew Brett wouldn't do anything like that, she was bubbling inside. I knew he wouldn't——

'——and told me he was flattered that a woman who loved her husband as much as I do would choose him as a weapon. Actually,' Gwen mused, 'he was quite charming about it. He could have asked what I thought he could possibly see in a sagging mother of two! He's really a wonderful guy, Rebecca——'

Rebecca pulled herself together with an effort. 'Why are you telling me about Brett?' she asked, trying to keep her voice light.

Gwen raised a speculative eyebrow. 'Because I assumed that was the other half of the secret,' she said crisply, 'and that you'd feel better if you knew he hadn't been messing around with your sister.'

Rebecca shook her head. 'There is no other half of the secret.'

'Oh.' Gwen looked glum. 'Well, I'm still glad you dumped Paul. I won't tell anyone till it's official; I can keep my mouth shut. And that reminds me—have you heard that the Mayor and the City Council will be meeting in closed session tomorrow afternoon at four?'

'What was that you said about keeping your mouth shut, Gwen?' Rebecca teased. Then, abruptly, she sobered. 'What do you mean, closed session? They can't do that. It's illegal.'

'According to our esteemed parent, they can, when they're discussing things that might encourage speculative investments. Things like land transfers, and——'

'They're actually going to do it, then. They're going to give that land to Brett Hilliard——'

'Are you really upset, Rebecca? You honestly haven't

changed your mind about Brett after all? I thought you'd
be glad to have the deal go through. You did go to
Chicago with him——'

'I did not! And if you say that around this town——'

'You know what I mean. I really thought you were
attracted to him.'

So attracted to him, Rebecca thought, that if he
doesn't want me, I will have to leave this town, because I
couldn't bear to be near him, and not be with him . . .
'Why does Brett want to come here, anyway?' she asked,
her fear making her irritable. 'Why Fultonsville? Does
he just want to be a big fish in a small pond?'

'You've got me,' Gwen said comfortably. 'Maybe he
likes the people.'

'He's already holding the hoop for everyone in town to
jump through, that's certain. Thanks for the tip, Gwen.
I'll go to the meeting tomorrow and see what happens.'

'Just don't tell Dad where you heard about it, or we'll
both be disowned,' Gwen laughed.

'That's no problem for you. You've got a husband to go
back to.' For the first time in her life, Rebecca realised,
she was the tiniest bit jealous of her sister.

Either Gwen hadn't heard the meeting time correctly, or
Ted Barclay had purposely given her the wrong hour.
Those were the only possibilities Rebecca could come up
with, because when she arrived at City Hall at fifteen
minutes to four the following afternoon, the Mayor's
secretary greeted her with a smile and told her that the
council was already in session.

'I'll wait,' Rebecca said sweetly.

The secretary's expression didn't alter. 'I'll get you a
cup of coffee. It may be a long meeting.'

'Is Mr Hilliard in the council-room?'

The secretary was immediately on guard. 'Of course
not.'

'Where is he?'

'He's waiting in the Mayor's office. But you can't go in there either. His Honour said no press——'

'I see.' The careless questions had achieved Rebecca's purpose; if Brett had been included in the meeting, she would have stormed in, demanding that the rest of the public be admitted. The secretary had obviously been on the lookout for that. But she had unwittingly given away a bit of information that was worth even more to Rebecca. If Brett was in Fultonsville at all, it meant that everyone expected the deal to go through. He would hardly have come down from Chicago for the privilege of being told no.

Brett's here, Rebecca thought, and tried very hard to discipline the wild joy that ran through her veins at the thought of seeing him again. She hadn't realised that she had missed him so much; looking back, the four days since she had seen him seemed endless.

The secretary gathered up a stack of papers. 'Rebecca,' she said, 'I need to take these forms down the hall, but your father told me to guard the door of the meeting-room with my life so you can't barge in. Now, if you'll give me your solemn word——'

Rebecca sipped her coffee and raised her right hand. 'I swear I will not interrupt the council meeting,' she promised.

'I knew I could trust you. I'll be back in a minute, and the Mayor will never know I've been gone, right?'

'Not from me. In fact, I may not even stick around,' Rebecca said carelessly. 'I've got better things to do than sit here while they talk.'

As soon as the secretary was out of sight, Rebecca drained her coffee-cup, set it on the corner of the desk where the woman couldn't miss it, and tiptoed across to the Mayor's private office.

Brett was lying on the couch, his fingers laced behind

his head, staring at the ceiling. He looked up as she came in.

'Well,' he said. 'You're a welcome sight. Did they send you in to keep me company, so I wouldn't notice how long it's taking to decide anything?' He sat up and patted the couch cushion beside him.

Rebecca ignored the invitation, though the caressing note in his voice sent her pulse-rate soaring. Business was business, she reminded herself. She closed the office door and perched on the corner of her father's massive desk. 'You seem very certain that the council is going to give you the deal you want,' she observed.

He raised an eyebrow. 'And how did you reach that conclusion?'

'You're here.'

'And you don't think there is anything else in Fultonsville that interests me?' It was soft, seductive. His eyes focused on her left hand, and then lifted, dark with anger, to her face. 'I see you're still engaged,' he said, his voice clipped and even. 'What the hell is the matter with you, Rebecca, that you came running back to him?'

Something snapped inside her, and she bit off the explanation that trembled on her lips. What good would it do to try to explain it to him? He had drawn his own conclusions. And why should she recite the details for Brett's personal pleasure? She owed Paul that much respect, at least—to keep private things private.

She raised her chin, stubbornly. 'Yes,' she said. 'I am still wearing his ring. And just what do you plan to do about it? I may have gone to bed with you in a moment of weakness, but that doesn't mean you own me!'

'Perhaps,' he said coolly, 'I should have a talk with a banker acquaintance of mine. Perhaps I should apologise to him for some things that happened last week——'

'You wouldn't dare,' Rebecca said. Her voice trembled just a little.

'Wouldn't I? I don't have anything to lose. Perhaps I

should tell Paul all about his future bride,' he said. 'He might like to know some of the things that I discovered——'

'Please, Brett. There is no need to be crude.'

'You know,' he said thoughtfully, 'I've always made it a rule to stay away from married women. They're generally more trouble than they're worth. But for you, Rebecca, I'll make an exception.'

And that, she thought, is all I mean to him. He doesn't care if I marry Paul or not, as long as it doesn't interfere with his pleasure. 'And just what makes you think I'd be interested in having an affair with you?'

There was no humour in his smile. 'Shall I demonstrate?'

She interrupted firmly, determined not to lose control of the conversation. 'Win or lose,' she said, 'I'd like to have you on the show tomorrow to talk about your plans.'

'All of them? Isn't this a family show?'

'Dammit, Brett——'

'Oh, you mean just about the business.' His tone was bitingly ironic. 'Certainly—it will be good public relations for the company. Are you sure you don't want to run a special tonight? The news would be fresher.'

'Tomorrow will be good enough. I have other plans for tonight.'

He glanced at his watch. 'Paul, I suppose. Tell me, did you confess the whole thing to him—suitably edited, of course? And did he forgive you? And did you promise never to do it again?'

She didn't respond.

'Perhaps we should have him come over now and play chaperon. I'm sure you'd feel more comfortable with him here. The council members might not finish their little chat till bedtime—you wouldn't happen to have a pack of playing cards, would you?'

'Why?' Rebecca asked tartly. 'Were you going to suggest strip poker?' She bit her tongue, sorry that the

comment had escaped. Why climb down into the gutter
with him?

He grinned. 'What a wonderful idea.'

'Sorry. I don't carry cards.'

'Really? You seem to have everything else in that
bag.'

'You'd be amazed how much I've removed since I had
to live without it for a few days.'

'I guess we'll have to come up with some other ideas,
then.'

'Leave me out of this, please. I don't need to be
entertained.'

'What a spoil-sport you are,' he murmured. 'And I was
thinking of all those wonderful ways I've found of
amusing you.'

Rebecca swallowed hard. She had overestimated
herself, she realised, and forgotten how easily he could
make her remember the mindless magic they had made
together. If only it was real, she thought painfully, and
not just a game we were playing—a hurtful game. She
said stiffly, 'I could just tape the interview for tomorrow,
if you'd rather not waste the time to come to the station.'
And then, she thought, I can get out of here, and go
home . . .

For a moment, he seemed not to hear. He was
watching her closely, his gaze roaming over her body.
She tried to pretend it wasn't happening.

He rose lazily and came across the room to her. 'As a
matter of fact,' he said, 'it won't be a waste of time if I
can sit and stare at you, Rebecca.'

'Be serious, Brett.'

'I am very serious. Do you still think the council is
going to turn me down?'

'Obviously, you don't.'

'I suppose, if they decide to go ahead, you'll use the
whole two hours of the show tomorrow to rake me over
the coals again.'

'No.' He looked startled, and she stumbled to explain. 'I don't suppose you've heard the story I did after last weekend?'

'No. Do you mean it was favourable?'

'I think you'd find it so. And don't get any ideas about why I wrote it that way, either!' she bristled.

He shook his head. 'I'm amazed.'

'I still think the council is moving too quickly, but what can I accomplish by fighting the inevitable?'

'I wish I really believed that you would remember that,' he murmured. He was standing close to her by then. She could feel the hairs on her arms rising, as if there were some freaky kind of static electricity between them.

'I promise you, Rebecca, I'll do my best to be a good citizen of Fultonsville.' His voice was almost a caress, despite the commonplace words.

She tried to shake off the mood. 'Is that the best you can do for a statement to the press, Mr Hilliard? Nothing more original than that?'

'There are several things I'd like to say to the press—or at least to this particular reporter.' He braced his hands on the desk, one on each side of her, so closely that she could feel the warmth of his fingers even though he wasn't actually touching her. His body formed a sort of trap, holding her prisoner on the desk. 'I'm tired of talking about business, Rebecca. Let's stop playing games. We both know what's really going on here——'

Her breath was coming a little faster than normal.

'I'd like to tell you that you're beautiful, and that you seriously disturbed my sleep all weekend. Why did you leave Chicago, Rebecca?'

'My job was done.'

'It was more than that, and you know it. There were things I wanted to show you—things I wanted to do with you——'

His voice was intimate, husky. It was like a sharp

fragment of ice sliding up and down her spine, leaving no doubt about the kind of things he had intended to do. She stared at the wall over his shoulder and tried to shut out that persuasive voice, reminding herself that he still thought she had come back to Paul. He's setting you up, she told herself.

'Doesn't it ever make you wonder?' he asked. 'Did you lie awake all weekend, too, wishing that you were in my arms again?'

'No, I didn't,' she said firmly, and was uncomfortably aware that it wasn't the truth.

'So you've gone back to him,' he said. 'You won't be happy there, you know. If you were really content with Paul, you wouldn't be playing these games with me.'

Furious colour flamed in her face. 'You accuse me of playing games! You're the one who——'

His hands brushed her hips, her waist, her breasts, kindling the now-familiar fire, and even if she could have remembered what it was she wanted to say, she couldn't have shaped the words.

This time, passion was accompanied by a twinge of terror. I was never going to let him touch me again, she thought. This is dangerous. This is like playing with a hand grenade. She closed her eyes, trying to shut out the danger.

'You're an expert at games, you see,' he whispered. 'At this very moment you're waiting to be kissed, sitting there with your eyes closed so that you can pretend you didn't see it coming. Then you can play the innocent with Paul——'

His mouth was a brand that sealed off the protest she tried to make, smothering the unspoken words. She tried to fight him off, but she was fighting herself as well, her own traitorous desire to let the flames rise up and consume her——

He raised his head, breathing hard. 'Does your pretend banker make you feel like this, Rebecca?'

'Don't call him that.'

'That's what he is. He's a man without ambition, riding on his father's influence——'

'You're part of a family business, too!' she flared. But as soon as the words were spoken, she recognised the unfairness of what she had said. Brett was a Hilliard, all right, and that had given him his start. But it wasn't his name alone that had won devotion and loyalty from his employees.

'Paul will never be anything but his father's errand boy.' It was flat, final. 'You don't want him, Rebecca. You know, in your heart, that you don't——'

'I don't want you either!' It was childish, she knew, but she felt that she had to strike out at him, to hurt him, to stop him from saying these things to her. He had no right to interfere with her life like this——

'Perhaps you don't. But your insatiable curiosity won't let you rest. You want to know. You can't be loyal to Paul; it isn't in your nature.'

She tried to push him away, but it was like iron filings trying to escape a magnet. He held her easily, his hands spread across her back, holding her firmly. 'You don't really want to escape, Rebecca. You want me to hold you, so that you can blame me.' There was a vaguely threatening note in his voice. 'Is safety what you really want? How long do you think it will be before Rebel reappears, and blows your marriage vows into fragments? You have to be true to yourself, or come apart at the seams. And it's impossible for you to be loyal to both Paul and yourself, when the two things are opposites.'

She turned her back on him, staring out of the window at the traffic on the street. 'Why are you saying these things to me? What makes you think it's your business what I do?'

'Because what happened to us in Chicago wasn't a one-time thing, Rebecca. You're going to end up in bed with me, whether you marry Paul or not. I'd just as soon avoid the mess. Break it off, Rebecca, for his sake as well as yours——'

'And start sleeping with you instead?' Her voice was bitter. How dared he think that she had so little strength of character that she couldn't be true to a marriage vow! The sudden impulse to hurt him was more than she could bear. 'Perhaps I went to bed with you just to see what it was like, Brett. You're so convinced that you're the world's greatest lover that you're imagining things——'

His eyes were black sparks. She had never seen him so angry, and she shrank back on the corner of the desk, desperate to escape the effects of his fury. If she made herself small enough, she thought frantically, perhaps he would forget that she was there . . .

His hands fell on her shoulders, and he dragged her off the desk and into his arms, roughly. 'My imagination, is it?' he asked. 'Am I imagining the way you can't get your breath?' He brushed the curtain of red-gold hair aside and sought the pulse point at the base of her throat. 'It seems to me your heart is racing, Rebecca—but tell me, am I imagining that as well? And this——'

'Don't,' she whimpered.

His hand brushed across her breast, against her will the nipple tightened under the casual contact. 'Is this only in my imagination, too?' His fingertips probed the tender flesh. 'You can't do this, Rebecca. You can't tease a man to distraction, and then tell him that he was mistaken—that he made it all up. Dammit, Rebecca, you can't make me believe this isn't real!'

He forced her chin up, till she had no choice but to look straight at him. What she saw in his eyes terrified her. It wasn't violence, though for a moment she had been afraid that she might have pushed him to that point. Even the anger was dying as she stared up at him.

No matter what, she thought, I want him now, for as long as he will stay with me. That is all that matters to me now . . .

He saw the softness come into her face. With a groan, he pulled her close.

It was a different kind of kiss, a hungry, soul-searing caress that seemed to reach down deep inside Rebecca and pull her heart up by the roots. Common sense had long vanished. Right now, it didn't seem to matter, so long as nothing took her out of Brett's arms.

She sighed, a little animal sound, and pressed herself more closely against him.

The office door opened. Rebecca heard it, but the sound didn't quite register. She was smiling, her face flushed with the pleasure of his kisses, and nothing else seemed quite real. Then, from the corner of her eye, she saw something that had not been there before—something that looked like her father's favourite tartan sports jacket, and she turned her head to see what had reminded her of that awful pattern . . .

For ten full seconds no one moved, not the couple in the office, nor the Mayor and council members at the door.

She closed her eyes in pain. But she could not shut out the sight of six faces, staring at her with varying degrees of interest, shock, and amazement.

'Rebecca?' Her father's astonished voice was a mere squeak. He coughed, and cleared his throat. 'Well,' he said, with a twinge of good humour creeping back into his tone. 'Am I hallucinating, or have you two settled your differences?'

CHAPTER TEN

BRETT'S hold on her had loosened. Rebecca stepped away from him and stopped short, as though drawn up by a leash. Pain was shooting through her scalp. For a moment, she didn't even know what had happened; her whole body hurt, as if she had been beaten, and the soreness in her scalp was mild by contrast.

'Hold on,' Brett said. He sounded a little breathless. 'You've got a lock of hair wound around my watch band.'

She shifted impatiently from one foot to the other while he untangled the red-gold strands, too much aware of the touch of his fingers to stand still. She kept her head bent so that she didn't have to look at that circle of astonished faces. If I don't look at them, she was thinking, maybe it won't have happened. If I explain to them that it was an accident, perhaps they won't tell anyone——

But she knew better. There would be no rescue from the consequences, because this was too good a story for anyone to keep secret. This time, her luck had run out.

Oh, God, she thought. When the rumour-mongers get hold of this one, they're going to have a wonderful time! The story of Rebecca Barclay and Brett Hilliard being caught kissing in the Mayor's office would fly, and probably grow larger as it was retold. She didn't even want to think about how tall the tale might get.

Paul is coming home today, she thought with a sickening thud in the pit of her stomach. She still had to tell Paul. She must get to him, and explain it, before the rumours reached him. She owed it to him to hurt him as little as possible . . .

In the meantime, since there was no sense in denying

158

what had happened—the six astounded men did, after all, know what they had seen—and no possible way to explain it, she might as well take a leaf out of her father's instruction manual and act as a good politician would. If she pretended that the incident wasn't important, they might believe that it wasn't. Back to business, Rebecca, she told herself firmly. It would take their minds off what they had seen, and that would be good for both her and Brett. After all, she realised, the council might be a little disillusioned with his behaviour, as well.

'Do you have an announcement to make?' she asked her father. She could see Brett, from the corner of her eye. She thought she saw a flicker of surprise cross his face.

Ted Barclay shifted uneasily. 'We're going to call a press conference in an hour or two,' he said. 'Until then, Rebecca, I simply can't give you anything——'

'You can't stop me from speculating about what went on in the meeting,' she pointed out.

He sighed. 'I see I'm talking to the reporter again, and not my daughter.'

'Dad, you know I'll go to any lengths to get the story.' Her voice held a tinge of bitterness, and she looked directly at Brett as she went on. 'No matter what it takes. Be sure to call me about the press conference.' She picked up her handbag.

Her father said quietly, 'It took a little longer than I expected, Brett. Sorry about the delay.' His eyes followed Rebecca to the door. 'Don't mind her,' he said. 'She gets this way sometimes when she's chasing a story. It's the only thing that matters.'

She didn't turn around. She squared her shoulders. It was better that way, she told herself, than if her father suspected the truth.

'Rebecca——' Brett followed her into the hallway. 'Give me a minute with them, and then I'll come with you, and we'll get this straightened out.'

She frowned, puzzled. 'And just where do you think I'm going?'

'To talk to Paul, of course.'

She shivered a little at the idea. It would be hard enough, to do it by herself, but to have Brett there . . . 'I don't need your help.'

He put out a gentle hand to touch the tumbled hair. 'Nevertheless,' he murmured, 'I want to be there with you.'

She jerked away. 'Haven't you done enough damage?' she snapped. 'Or do you just want a ringside seat, so that you can enjoy watching the results of all the hard work you've done to mess up my life?'

His face had hardened. 'So you're going to try to explain it to him,' he said harshly. 'Yes, I'd like to see that.'

'If you would only listen to me——'

'I wouldn't be surprised if you can pull it off, if you manage to persuade Paul that the whole thing was only a mistake, and wheedle him into forgiving you and going on with the wedding. But is that what you really want, Rebecca? A husband you can manipulate so easily? A man who probably wouldn't even notice whether you were unfaithful to him!'

Her eyes blurred till the stripes on his tie looked like ocean waves. 'Damn you, Brett! You're so certain that you're always right that you won't even listen——'

'Brett——' Ted Barclay spoke from the office door.

'Just a minute, Ted!' There was irritation in Brett's voice. 'Can't you see——'

'I see that both you and Rebecca need a little time to cool off, before either of you does anything you'll regret.'

Rebecca thought that sounded like good advice. If she acted on her impulses right now, she would murder Brett Hilliard, and though at the moment she couldn't imagine ever regretting it, she supposed it would be just as well to wait a day or two.

She looked up at Brett for an instant, and then she turned away.

'Let her go,' she heard her father say. 'She has to do this herself. You'll only make it harder for her.'

Paul, she thought. She walked down Main Street towards the radio station. He would be back any time now, and she had no idea what she was going to tell him. It would have been difficult enough without this last scene . . .

'I'll confess it all,' she muttered. 'As soon as I've filed my story, I'll go and find him and tell him everything, before the rumours have a chance to reach him. He'll understand. He simply has to understand that I can't go on.'

She walked across the small park in the centre of town, past the bubbling fountain, past the bandstand. The autumn flowers were in full array, the showy beds of asters and zinnias gleaming yellow and gold at the edges of the park. Their strong scent, intensified by the heavy, humid air, tugged at her senses. It made her wish that she was back in the sleepy days of early summer, before Brett Hilliard had come to Fultonsville and so thoroughly upset her life.

Her step slowed as she reached the street again. She had to get herself together and get some sort of organisation to her thoughts before she burst into the station and tried to put a story about the council meeting on the air. She tried out one sentence after another in her head, and didn't like any of them. The thought of Paul kept intruding, and the hard cynicism of Brett's face as she had turned away from him.

Then she bumped headlong into a man on the pavement and nearly went sprawling. He caught her and set her back on her feet. 'They told me at the station that you were at City Hall,' he said. 'I was just on my way over to find you.'

'Paul,' she whispered. 'I didn't realise you were back.'

She almost didn't recognise him. He wasn't wearing a jacket, the long sleeves of his shirt were untidily rolled to the elbow, and his tie was askew. He looked very hot and very angry.

'I just got back into town,' he said, 'and you won't believe what I've been told.'

'Oh, no,' Rebecca said, under her breath. I knew rumours travelled fast in this town, she told herself, but I had no idea that it could exceed the speed of light!

Unless Brett had done this to her——

Slow suspicion started to grow. The only way Paul could have heard about this disaster so quickly was if someone had called him at the bank. The council members would have had no reason to do that; they would have been content to tell their wives the new bit of gossip over dinner. And her father certainly wouldn't have done such a thing; hadn't he told Brett there in the hall outside his office that Rebecca must deal with this herself?

But Brett had given her no chance to explain that she only wanted to talk to Paul alone, that of course she didn't still intend to marry him. And Brett had every reason to want Paul to know about this latest disaster.

Brett, she thought, and fury began to build in her. What in the hell makes him think he can tell me what to do? she raged inside. Did he enjoy playing with her life as if it was a stack of children's blocks, building up towers and then knocking them down purely for entertainment?

'Rebecca,' Paul said. 'I scarcely know what to think——'

'I don't blame you for being angry with me,' she said drearily.

'Then it *was* you?'

'Was there any doubt? Paul, I can explain——'

'I'd like to see you try,' he said fiercely. 'What kind of explanation can there possibly be? Rebecca, we're engaged to be married, and you were seen kissing Brett Hilliard.'

'Well, yes, but——'

'I suppose you're going to tell me that he grabbed you against your will and assaulted you!'

She sighed. 'Not exactly.'

'As far as I'm concerned, there is no accounting for this—this aberration!'

'Paul, we're standing in the middle of the street——'

'From what I've been hearing,' he pointed out, 'publicity doesn't seem to bother you.'

Rebecca bit her lip and went on. 'Paul, I did tell you last weekend that I wanted to break our engagement. I meant it then, and I mean it now.'

'You have gone completely out of your mind, Rebecca!'

'Please, Paul. Could you come over later so we can talk about this?'

'Why not now? Do you need time to cook up a cover story?'

She didn't blame him for being angry. 'Of course not. I just thought that we'd get farther if we could talk about it quietly, without interruption——'

'I don't think I'm capable of that,' he admitted. 'And I doubt if putting it off till later tonight would make any difference whatsoever. My mother warned me that you weren't the kind of girl you seemed, but I thought she was wrong, Rebecca.'

'I should have known your mother would come into it,' she snapped, unable to stay still.

'My mother is quite sincere,' he said stiffly. 'She has my best interests at heart.'

'I've never questioned that for an instant. But I thought you had different ideas about what you wanted. Now, can we talk about this or not? If you want to take care of it right now, fine. But could we go somewhere quiet?'

'Why? Union Station suited you just fine when it was Hilliard.'

'I can explain what happened today——' At least I hope I can, she thought. Then she realised what he had said. 'You know about Union Station, too?' she asked, in a harsh whisper.

'What do you mean, too? I know that a friend of my mother saw you kissing Hilliard on the platform as if one of you was being shipped off to war. What else is there to know, Rebecca?'

She put her fingertips on her aching temples, and wondered if it was possible to think herself into a fatal stroke right there on the pavement.

'My mother thought it was a cute story about someone who looks like you,' he went on. 'Of course, she didn't know that you actually came home on Friday night on that train. I shudder to think of what she'll have to say if she ever finds out.'

Rebecca scarcely heard him. If he hasn't even heard about the latest episode, she thought, and he's furious already, then there is no way that he's going to listen to anything I have to say. I can't possibly make him understand that I didn't do it on purpose, that what I feel for Brett is beyond my control . . .

She looked up at him, as if she hadn't seen him in a long time. The red-flushed face, the weak chin that didn't show when he was smiling—she hadn't ever seen him quite this angry before. He wasn't like that; he didn't get furious. He was always willing to listen.

Well, this time he wasn't. She felt the tiniest twinge of humour; Brett had been wrong about one thing, at least. Paul was not as easily manipulated as he had expected.

She felt the merest flutter of relief deep inside her, relief that this part of her life was over. There would be no argument from Paul about pre-wedding jitters this time! And while she would have much preferred settling it quietly and calmly, she couldn't bring herself to regret that now she didn't have to explain anything at all.

'I'm waiting, Rebecca,' Paul reminded curtly.

She stared up at him, and then she tugged the diamond ring off her finger. 'I don't think there is any point in discussing it, Paul. Why don't we do it this way, and then I don't owe you any explanations?'

'Rebecca!' He sounded horrified. 'Do you mean that it was bad enough to make you break off our engagement——'

'Paul, we haven't been engaged since Friday night, so what I do is really none of your business any more, is it?' She put the ring into his hand and closed his fingers over it. 'I'm sorry it happened this way.'

'Rebecca——'

'It's for the best, believe me.'

He looked down at the ring, sparkling in his palm. 'I suppose that perhaps it is.'

'I'm sorry I hurt you. But we wouldn't have suited, Paul.' She turned away, the news report for the station forgotten.

She skipped the press conference at City Hall. She knew that her absence would only add fuel to the already-raging fire of rumour, but she couldn't bear to face Brett again today. She needed to think things through first. She hoped he would realise that, and not turn up on her doorstep, expecting a conquering hero's welcome.

Conquering hero, indeed, she thought. If he had the nerve to show up at her apartment, expecting her to throw herself into his arms——

'I probably will do just that,' she admitted wryly. After that blinding realisation in his arms, there in her father's office, there was only one answer she could give him. She would do anything, promise anything he wanted——

She made herself a pot of tea and curled up in the window-seat in the tiny tower off her living-room. From there, she could watch the street and be warned of his approach.

But he didn't come at all, and that made her even more angry. He had told her, outside her father's office, that he wanted to come with her, to talk things out. Had he only been saying that to soothe her, knowing that he couldn't possibly leave the council just then, no matter what she said?

Perhaps he hadn't planned the little scene in Ted Barclay's office after all, she thought. He might have been only indulging himself in a harmless bit of fun by kissing her—an interesting way to pass the time while he waited. Perhaps he had been just as embarrassed by it as she had, and now he had no intention of letting the game go any further. Was that what he had intended to talk to her about? Had all his talk about not making love to a married woman been only a line? He had seemed awfully certain that she intended to marry Paul, despite everything . . .

Fury started to build deep inside her. He doesn't like reporters, she remembered. Peggy Williams had told her that, in that stuffy little apartment in Chicago. Rebecca had seen that dislike for herself, well hidden though it was, the first time she had interviewed him. And yet, Brett had sought her out, had invited her to come to the city. Why? she wondered. Had it been, as she had believed, an honest effort to convert an opponent to his way of thinking? Or had he intended from the beginning to destroy her, just for the fun of getting even with one member of the profession he disliked?

'Not Brett,' she whispered, scarcely aware of the sound of her voice in the quiet room. 'Brett isn't vindictive. He wouldn't take his revenge on me just because of my job.'

How far she had come, she realised with a twinge of panic, from the way she had felt about him just a few weeks before. Then, she had been convinced he was a corporate con artist, determined to bleed Fultonsville of all the advantages it held for him, and then, at his convenience, move on to another town and another set of credulous officials who would do anything they could to bring an industry to town.

Now, she thought, she knew the essential man, the gentle, private one who didn't talk about himself, but whose actions shouted in even the quietest room.

He wasn't an easy man to know. It had been a challenge to figure him out, like fitting together the pieces of a shattered china plate. At first she had had only the bits of the rim—the public face of the man, enough to see the shape of him, but not enough to know what he really was. She had discovered him slowly, picking up fragments from his employees, from his friends, from watching him as he worked and as he played.

If I know him for fifty years, she thought, I'll still find new pieces now and then.

But would she see him again at all? He'd had his fun, he'd accomplished his purpose. He might never come back at all, for fear that she might take him seriously, and—now that her engagement was at an end—expect that he would want to marry her.

'You're incapable of being faithful to Paul,' Brett had told her once. A man who thought that of her wasn't about to propose marriage himself, she told herself sadly. If he thought that she would cheat on her marriage vows, he might want to be her lover, but not her husband.

And, she reminded herself, she had built that trap with her own two hands. She had played the dangerous game, let herself be involved in those public scenes. She had no one to blame but herself.

I never thought I was a self-destructive personality, she mused. I take care of my health, I fasten my seat-belt, I don't gamble, and I've never even contemplated suicide. But apparently I like to flirt with danger in other ways. I'm not content with safety, and I've nearly wrecked my life and my reputation to avoid getting stuck with security.

It was a sobering thought. 'Maybe Brett can explain it to me,' she said. She would have to see him some time, she reflected. In a town the size of Fultonsville, he couldn't possibly avoid her.

If, that is, he stayed in Fultonsville, she thought. She hadn't gone to the press conference, hadn't heard a news report. She was assuming that the plans had been approved. But what if the City Council had decided against the investment?

'He said he'd be on my show tomorrow, win or lose,' she reminded herself. But that had been before—— She stopped there. She didn't even want to think about the minutes she had spent in his arms.

What if Brett had decided to cut his losses? What if he had gone already, back to Chicago, or on to the next town that might provide a new home for his business?

What if I don't see him again? she thought, in sudden panic. I can't stand it—I can't——

She jumped up from the window-seat and rushed to turn the television set on. But the evening news was past, and only a scratched old black and white movie filled the air waves. 'Damn,' she muttered. In the morning, she would know. But morning wasn't soon enough. Her heart was pounding, and she felt as if she couldn't get enough air into her lungs to sustain her. Was that why he hadn't come tonight? Because he wasn't even in town? And if Brett had gone, what did that mean for Rebecca?

'I'll call Dad,' she said, and had dialled the number before she slammed the telephone down again. Not that, she decided. She could do anything else, but she would not call up her father and beg for information. If she could be certain that Gwen would answer the phone— but she couldn't. And the embarrassment of admitting to her father that she didn't know what had happened, or where Brett was, would be too much for Rebecca to handle.

She called the radio station instead. The telephone

rang for what seemed for ever before the night disc jockey said, 'Yeah? Got a request?'

'Yes,' she said politely. 'This is Rebel. What did the City Council do today?'

'Is this a new riddle?'

'No. I'm serious. Did they give Hilliard the money, or not?'

'You mean you don't know?' The man sounded astonished. 'Where have you been all evening?'

'None of your business.'

'The whole town is celebrating down at the riverbank. The crowd decided a party was required, so they started the jazz festival a day early. The festival promoters are going nuts, but the crowd's having a wonderful time——'

Rebecca cut through the stream of talk. 'They said yes?'

'They sure did. The papers are signed. Why? Are you going to start a petition to impeach the Mayor? I wouldn't recommend you start at the riverbank; those people would lynch you.'

She closed her eyes in relief, and gently put the telephone down in the middle of the disc jockey's lecture.

So Brett was still in town, she reflected. And he would come to the studio tomorrow, and they would do the show——

And I will sit there next to him for two hours, she thought, and daydream about being in his arms again, and after the show——

After the show, she reminded herself, he might very well just walk away. After all, he could have sought her out, once the press conference was over, if he had still wanted to talk to her . . .

This pain will go away, she told herself. I'll get over it.

A moment later, incurable honesty forced itself upon her. Don't kid yourself, she warned. You'll never get over this one.

She dozed off there on the window-seat, and woke in the early morning to a cool mist flowing gently through the open window, as was common along the river in late summer. As the day progressed, the sun would burn off the fog, and the muggy heat would return. But for the moment, the air felt crisp, with a hint of autumn in it.

'I'll make a fresh start,' she told herself, and knew as she said it that the brave words would be hard to carry through.

She leaned a hot cheek against the coolness of the window pane, and for a moment thought that through sheer desire her mind had conjured up a vision of the man she so wanted to see.

He came up the pavement through the mist, as silently as a ghost, and with her first sight of him Rebecca's eyes widened, and her heart slammed itself into her ribs with sickening intensity.

It was one thing to sit in her quiet apartment and confess to herself that she loved him, that she would always love him. It was something else to see him again, and to know that without him her life had no meaning at all.

I've fallen so hard that I'll never get up again, she admitted painfully. I love him more than I've ever known it was possible to love . . .

CHAPTER ELEVEN

AND now what do I do? she asked herself wearily. He hadn't come last night. Did that mean he didn't want her love, her devotion?

I must not ask for promises, she told herself. Whatever he wants to give me—that will have to be enough.

She was waiting by the open door of her apartment when he came up the staircase. She wasn't quite sure how she had got there, or what she would say. He hesitated an instant on the final step, when he saw her.

She swallowed hard. 'It's early,' she said, with morning huskiness still in her voice. 'Would you like breakfast?'

He thought about it for an instant, and smiled. 'Yes, I would.' He closed the door behind them. 'That sounds very domestic, Rebecca.'

She searched the words and the tone for sarcasm, and found none. She kept her back turned, and reached into the refrigerator for eggs.

'You weren't at the press conference,' he said.

'No. But I heard.'

'And how do you feel about it?'

This is all wrong, she was screaming inside. It shouldn't be like this—a careful discussion of industrial development! 'I'm glad.' Her voice was carefully neutral.

'Are you?' He came across the room; she could hear his steps on the hard floor. She braced herself, but the touch of his hand on her hair, streaming unbrushed down her back, sent a shiver down her spine, a memory of how it had felt to lie in his arms, to feel his hands against her naked skin.

She wanted to throw herself into his arms then, but she was afraid that she would only make it worse.

171

He caught her hand as she reached for an omelette pan. 'No engagement ring,' he said.

She shook her head. She was afraid to speak. Would this be the breakthrough?

'Paul was at the festival last night,' he said. His voice was expressionless. 'He was drinking beer. He ended up standing on a table, announcing to anyone who would listen that you were the only woman in the world for him, and if you'd have him back, he'd marry you in a minute.'

He sounded as if he was reading a prepared statement, she thought, as if the words had no personal meaning at all.

'He was a little incoherent,' Brett went on, 'but I gathered that he thought he'd been unfair not to listen to your explanation of your erratic behaviour.'

'He probably thought it was a safe thing to say. I made it clear I don't plan to explain it.'

'Well, I wouldn't count on him actually doing anything about it. Considering the amount he'd had to drink, he probably won't remember a thing about last night.'

'I'm sorry for the hurt I caused him,' she murmured. She tried to break an egg, but her fingers were clumsy.

'Why didn't you try to make him understand, Rebecca?'

'Now you sound as if you want me to patch it up!' She was hurt, confused.

'I just want to be certain that you don't regret it.'

'I don't regret refusing to explain it. What could I have told him?' she asked, with irritation. 'I positively couldn't tell Paul the truth—and I'm not a good liar . . . I certainly couldn't have promised him that I'd never do it again——'

He turned her towards him, and when she tried to look away, he cupped her face in his hands so he could look down into her eyes.

A little tingle of dread raced along her bones. I want

him so much, she thought, but if he doesn't want me, I'm lost——

'I told Paul on Friday night that I wanted to break it off,' she said. Her words came fast and sharp, as if he might walk out at any moment. 'He wouldn't listen. Then he went out of town——' Her voice cracked.

There was a long silence, and then Brett said, very softly, in a voice that trembled just a little, 'So you wore his ring until you could convince him that you meant it?'

She nodded miserably. 'As far as I'm concerned, my engagement was over last Friday.' Why did I bother trying to explain, she thought. Every word of it is true, but that doesn't make it sound any less like a soap opera!

'Rebecca,' he said, and the last reserve crumbled. She pressed herself against him, hungry for the closeness that her body craved. There was no doubt left, no fear, just the overwhelming certainty that this was right, that it was inevitable.

I'll never know him completely, she thought. But to live with him would be a voyage of discovery. If I can have that, she told herself humbly, I'll ask nothing else of life . . .

He tasted her surrender, and demanded more, a response her starving soul was eager to give. She had thought his kisses powerful before, but now, with her last reservations gone, the energy that surged between them was more than she could bear. 'Please,' she whispered, scarcely aware that she had spoken.

He reached over her shoulder to turn off the heat under the small skillet. She was vaguely dissatisfied that he still had enough presence of mind to notice things like stoves left on, when she had forgotten everything of the kind. But then he picked her up to carry her into her bedroom, and she could no longer think at all.

Their lovemaking was slow and sensual, a space of time stolen from the commonplace world. Each stroke of his hands sent waves of desire slamming through her

body. All inhibition, all reservations dropped away, as
they shared the most powerful communication two
human beings can find, and drifted back to earth on the
soft ashes of their passion.

She nestled against him, her nose buried in the tanned
skin of his shoulder, content to lie there and breathe his
scent and let the slow rise and fall of his chest rock her
pleasantly.

Her hair had spilled across his chest, a tangled mass of
red-gold. He smoothed it into a web. 'Well?' he said. 'Did
that satisfy you, little kitten?'

Rebecca shook her head, without opening her eyes.
'No, I think you're going to have to explain it to me
again,' she murmured indistinctly.

'I'd be delighted—later. In the meantime, don't you
think you should call the station and tell them you're
taking the morning off, so they don't put out a missing-
person report on you?'

'In a little while.' She opened one eye and glanced at
the bedside clock. Then she sat up with a jerk. 'I had no
idea it was so late!'

'I thought your sense of time might have got a little
messed up,' Brett said pleasantly. 'Lucky your show isn't
till the afternoon.'

'I have to tape ads for Jack this morning. He's starting
a new promotional contest next week and I've got a
week's worth of work waiting for me.'

'Tell him you've got more important things to do.'

She paused on her way to the shower. 'If you don't like
it, you have only yourself to blame,' she pointed out. 'If I
hadn't spent two days last week in Chicago with
you——'

'And yesterday afternoon in the Mayor's office,' he
added smoothly, and laughed as embarrassed colour
splashed over her fair skin. 'How about lunch?'

She looked at the clock, and shook her head
reluctantly. 'I'm going to have enough trouble explaining

to Jack why I'm late. I won't dare leave till I've done the whole package.'

'I'd be happy to explain it to him,' Brett said lazily.

Rebecca's face flamed. She didn't answer, but once in the shower, she started to think about it. Just what would Brett have told Jack Barnes? What was the whole town going to think?

'It doesn't matter,' she told herself firmly, through the roar of the shower spray.

'What doesn't matter?' Brett put his head around the edge of the shower curtain.

She swallowed hard, unwilling to admit what she had been thinking. 'That we can't have lunch together today,' she said, finally. 'There will be another day.'

He smiled and leaned under the spray to kiss her. 'That's right,' he said against her lips, as water streamed over them both. 'There will be lots of days.'

She closed her eyes and swayed against him, her soapy hands slick against the muscles of his shoulders. The warm water pelting over her back and streaming down across her breasts was only an extension of the caress of his fingers against her sensitive skin.

'It's probably just as well that you're going to work,' he said huskily. 'If you didn't have to go, I'd drag you out of here and take you back to bed—wet and soapy or not. Though, come to think of it, why should I bother to drag you anywhere? I could just come in with you and——'

'Work?' she said hazily. 'What's work?'

Brett laughed, a little unsteadily. He turned her around under the shower spray, reached for the flannel, and started to massage her back with the rough-textured fabric. She sighed and relaxed under his hands, the brisk rubdown seeming more like an extended sensual caress. When he rinsed her off, kissed her lightly on the lips, and laid the flannel aside, she looked at him accusingly.

'This place has a good hot-water supply, I'll say that for it,' he murmured, and slapped her gently across the rear.

She reluctantly turned the taps off, climbed out of the shower, and wrapped herself in a towel. 'It's a nice place to live,' she said.

'You've told me that,' he said with a grin. 'That's why I came over this morning to talk to the landlord about his vacant apartment upstairs.' He kissed her nose. 'Can I use your phone this morning, Rebecca? It was too late last night to get things rolling, but I need to talk to my architect today.'

She nodded, woodenly, still feeling the weight of his words as if she had been hit by a truck, and he went off, whistling.

She rubbed her hair with a towel, hardly conscious of what she was doing. He didn't come to see me, she was thinking. He came here this morning to rent a lousy apartment, and I dragged him in here and practically seduced him——

Well, he certainly didn't seem to mind, she told herself irritably. Unfortunately, that didn't make the situation any less embarrassing.

My God, Rebecca, she thought. You've been blaming Brett for a week because he's made a fool of you, but you don't even need help—you can make yourself look like an idiot without even trying!

And what next, she asked herself. Would Brett thank her for the neighbourly welcome, and go on about his business? What a housewarming gesture for his new apartment!

He was talking on the telephone when she went back into her bedroom to get dressed. He had climbed back into bed and piled the pillows into a heap. His shoulders and chest were magnificently tan against the white sheets, and his hair, still damp from the shower, was starting to curl a little. He was carrying on a perfectly lucid conversation—giving instructions to his secretary, Rebecca thought—but his eyes never left her as she moved around the room, getting dressed. She hurried

into her clothes, and she thought that he looked a little
disappointed by her haste.

'The formal announcement will be made today,' he
was saying as Rebecca went back into the bathroom to
put on her make-up. 'You'll have to notify all the other
towns——'

I wonder, Rebecca thought, if his secretary has any
idea what he's doing. He's lying here in my bed, ogling
me while he's talking to her——

Oh, stop it, she told herself angrily. You went into this
with your eyes open, and now you shouldn't feel sorry for
yourself because it hurts. You knew it was going to.

She gave herself a brief lecture while she applied the
minimum of make-up, with a slightly shaky hand. When
she came out of the bathroom two minutes later, Brett
was sitting on the edge of the bed with his back to her.
'All right, I understand that he's being insistent,' he said.
'But now that we've decided on Fultonsville, it's out of
the question to move for another year at least . . .'

What did he mean, it was out of the question to move,
she wondered, her reporter's instincts aroused. But in a
year—just what was Brett planning to do next year?

'I don't need a public relations problem right now,'
Brett went on. He looked up then, and saw Rebecca.
'You can take care of it, I'm sure. Just do your best.'

This, Rebecca thought, was what she had feared all
along. He was already making arrangements to move on,
after the situation in Fultonsville lost its attractive
advantages.

And he's doing it from my bed, she thought bitterly.
The rotten double-crosser had got his promises, and
within twenty-four hours he was already planning to
violate his agreement with the town.

You don't know that, she reminded herself. You over-
heard half a conversation. But what other explanation
is there? As soon as he saw you, he started talking in
circles, as if he didn't want you to hear. At the minimum,

she decided, Brett had a bit of explaining to do.

She glanced at the clock and reached for her straw hat and handbag.

Brett looked up. He smiled at her and said into the phone, 'Wait a second.' He cupped his hand over the mouthpiece and said, 'You look absolutely delicious.'

Rebecca ignored the compliment. 'Don't forget the show,' she reminded. 'Just pull the door shut behind you when you leave—it'll lock itself.'

He looked a little startled. But Rebecca didn't give him a chance to question. She would do the questioning, she told herself, on the air this afternoon. And he had better have some answers.

Rebecca was in the broadcast-booth when he arrived five minutes before air time. She was checking the programme log to see what special features had to be fitted into her time-slot today, and arranging the taped cartridges in order. She had her pencil clenched between her teeth, and when Brett stooped to kiss her, she didn't remove it. He raised one smooth dark eyebrow, and kissed her cheek instead. 'No romance in the broadcast-booth?' he asked, and sat down in the chair reserved for her guests.

'No room, and no time,' she pointed out.

He chuckled, and looked around. 'Claustrophobia must be an occupational hazard,' he pointed out.

'Get everything settled with your secretary?' Rebecca asked.

'The architects are on the job. We'll break ground in a matter of weeks, and have the building up before winter—with all going well.'

'I'm sure my listeners will be delighted to hear about it.'

He tapped his fingers on the table-top, and said, 'Rebecca, what in the hell hit you? One minute you were an insatiable little sex kitten. Sixty seconds later you'd frozen into the next ice age, and I haven't the least idea what happened. Is it because I didn't get off the telephone to kiss you goodbye properly?'

'Something like that,' she said, without looking at him.

'That means you don't want to answer.'

'You're right on the ball, aren't you, Brett?'

'You're upset because I talked to her instead of kissing you goodbye? How about if we take care of the omission right now?' He pushed his chair back.

'We've only got two minutes to air time.'

'So I'll spend it kissing you.'

She made a meaningless note in the margin of the programme log. 'Go right ahead, if you insist. And you can consider it goodbye, too.'

'Rebecca, what in the devil does that mean?'

'It means that I don't appreciate being lied to, and used——'

'Are you saying that I've lied to you?' He sounded baffled.

The speaker on the wall squawked into life. 'Sixty seconds, Rebel.'

'Yes, you've lied to me! You said you would stay here, that the Fultonsville plant wasn't just a stepping-stone. But this morning you were talking to your secretary about how to keep the other towns happy and on the string, that you'll talk to them again in a year! And you had the nerve to say that in front of me—as if I'd keep quiet about it just because you took me to bed——'

The sweep second-hand on the big clock crossed the hour, and Rebel plugged in the cartridge that held her theme music. She took two deep breaths, and said, 'Welcome to *Rebel with a Cause* on this hot and muggy Tuesday afternoon. They always told me it wasn't the heat that was the bad part about living in the Midwest, it was the humidity—and on a day like today, there is no arguing with that conclusion. Of course, Fultonsville is a pretty hot place to be today in several ways, and my guest

today is one of the men who's helping to make it hot. He's
Brett Hilliard, who announced last night that Hilliard
Confectioners will be building a factory here in town. Of
course, that will be done with the considerable help of the
city itself——' her eyes met his, with an angry snap,
'——in the form of a gift of land, a building erected to Mr
Hilliard's specifications, and interest-free payments for a
number of years, in return for promises made by the
company. We'll be right back to discuss those promises
with Mr Hilliard after these messages.'

She pushed the button to start a taped advertisement,
and leaned back in her chair.

'Oh,' he said quietly, 'so that's what's been eating you.'

'Don't act so damned surprised! Or did you think
you'd been talking quietly enough that I couldn't hear
you?'

'You could have asked what was going on.'

'And got another snow job? I'm tired of your
explanations, Brett.'

'Then I'm not going to try to explain. It comes down to
an issue of trust, Rebecca. Do you trust me, or don't you?
You say I'm a con artist who's planning to play hopscotch
across Illinois, stealing from every town that will listen to
my pitch. If you've got any evidence to support that, I'd
like to hear it. I've put up with a lot from you, but not
even you can publicly call me a thief without backing up
your claim.'

'Not even me?' she whispered. Did she trust him? I
want to, she thought. And yet—I heard what he said, she
told herself. I heard it!

The tape ended and recycled itself, ready for the next
use. 'Welcome to *Rebel with A Cause*, Mr Hilliard.'

'Thank you.' He didn't give her a chance to continue.
'I'd like to address a rumour that seems to be circulating,
a rumour to the effect that I've already made plans to
take advantage of Fultonsville's generosity as long as it
lasts and then move my company to another location.

That rumour is vicious and vile, and absolutely untrue. I'd like to tell you and your listeners today that my commitment to Fultonsville is a lifetime one. I have every intention of growing old in this town, with a factory out there on the plain, growing and expanding and producing the best chocolate this country's ever seen.'

For an instant, Rebecca was speechless. Her throat was tight. Vicious and vile, was she? she thought. That was what he had called the idea, and they both knew that what he was really talking about was her.

He must have seen the confusion in her eyes, the stunned surprise that he had dared to take his case to the public. It might be just a clever public relations stunt, she told herself. And yet, there was no denying the angry ring of truth in his voice; no actor could fake that.

The telephone lines were lighting up. Still, Rebecca couldn't find her voice, and dead air time stretched out in an endless web. Every instant that went by made it harder to speak.

She had to say something. A chasm yawned in front of her; if she said the wrong word, she would tumble into it, down into the void. Trust—it's an issue of trust, he had said. Could she find it in her heart to put her faith completely in him?

I'm afraid, she thought. Afraid that if I trust him, he'll hurt me. But if I really love him—well, isn't that what love is? To put aside fear, and learn trust?

She looked up at him, and put a hand out blindly. 'Now that the decision is made,' she said, softly, 'it's time for all of us to pull together for the future of our town. And any doubts that some of us might still hold must be put aside, to give Brett and his employees a fair chance to make this new factory work.'

He smiled, a little, and his fingers closed round hers, a warm and comforting grip. 'Not exactly a gracious apology,' he murmured, 'but it will do.'

The phone calls started then. The callers asked him about employment, and expansion, and about whether the new people were enthusiastic about coming to Fultonsville. Brett answered each question with ease and good humour, never letting go of Rebecca's hand. She made a face at him, but he pretended not to understand, and he simply tightened his grip on her fingers.

She punched the button for the next call. It was awkward, running the control-board one-handed, and yet she could hardly come straight out and tell him to let her go.

She reached for a scrap of paper, scrawled a few words on it, and pushed it across the table to him. He looked at it with a frown, then wrote, *Sorry—can't read your handwriting* and pushed it back. She stuck her tongue out at him. He only smiled.

A quavery old voice said, 'Hello, Rebel, honey.'

'Hi, Mrs Henderson. Do you have a question for my guest, today?'

'Yes, I do. We've been hearing all about the business, but I want to know if he's a family man.'

Rebel rolled her eyes, but Brett only smiled. 'Mrs Henderson, I'd love to be. But I haven't found a woman yet who thinks I'm suitable material to be a husband.'

'None of them have ever been able to catch up with you long enough to find out, more likely,' Rebel muttered under her breath.

'What was that, honey? Mr Hilliard, aren't you at least bringing a pretty secretary with you?'

'Sorry to disappoint you, Mrs Henderson, But I'm not.'

Rebecca wondered if he meant that his secretary wasn't pretty, or that she wasn't coming with him. She couldn't get the sound of that woman's voice—pleasant, firm, giving nothing away—out of her head.

'I'll miss my secretary a great deal, but she has opted to take the early-retirement option we offered.' His eyes met Rebecca's. 'She's fifty-three,' he added gently.

Mrs Henderson made a gentle clucking sound. 'That's too bad.'

Rebel grabbed for the slip of paper. *You said you had a date with her*, she wrote furiously.

Brett looked at it with raised eyebrows. Then he said, very softly, 'Her son's a violinist with the symphony, and we went to a concert. Are you jealous?'

Mrs Henderson was prattling on. 'It's a shame our Rebel is already engaged.'

Of course I'm not jealous! Rebel wrote back.

He merely grinned at her and said, smoothly, 'Oh, didn't you know, Mrs Henderson? Rebel's broken her engagement.'

Rebel put her head down on the table. She wanted to scream, You can't do this to me on the air! I know that unexpectedness is part of what I like about the radio business, but this is ridiculous!

'Well, now, fancy that,' the old lady said. 'You should take her out, Mr Hilliard. I think you'd find you had a lot in common. And if you were to marry a local girl, why you'd feel ever so much more comfortable——'

Rebecca cut in, neatly. 'It's nice that everyone is concerned about making you comfortable here, Brett. Thanks for calling, Mrs Henderson. We've got time for just a couple more calls——'

'What about it, Rebecca?'

She tried to smile at him, to show how much she appreciated the joke.

'I think Mrs Henderson has a good idea,' he said. 'Will you marry me and make me feel comfortable in my new home town?'

She said, under her breath, 'That is not funny.' Before he had a chance to pursue it she had punched in the next caller.

Her heart was pounding. How she wished it was true, she realised. Maybe some day, she told herself with fierce longing, it might not be a joke. Some day, she might be his wife . . .

The show wound up quickly, and Rebecca was relieved when she was able to say, 'I think we've answered all the questions, Brett——'

'I have,' he interrupted. 'You haven't. Are you going to marry me, Rebecca?'

'You're turning my show into a soap opera,' she muttered.

Brett grinned. 'Tune in again tomorrow, folks, for the answer——'

She cut his microphone off the air. 'I should have done that fifteen minutes ago,' she said tartly, as soon as she had switched the responsibility back to the disc jockey in the control-room.

'Be a sport, Rebecca. When have I had a chance to talk to you?'

'Obviously not this morning. I didn't give you a chance to say much,' she admitted. Embarrassed colour washed over her face at the memory.

'Did I complain?' He reached for her. 'Let's go somewhere quiet——'

'Just a minute. There's something I have to ask first. Brett, I do trust you. I mean, I believe that you really mean to stay here. But——' She bit her lip. 'Would you tell me what you were talking about this morning?' She watched him out of the corner of her eye. 'I mean, if you weren't planning to leave——'

'Then why did I tell my secretary that I'd talk to the guy in another year? He's got a new candy bar he wants me to try, but it's going to take a year just to get this factory built and operating, making the products we already produce. I don't want to take on any new projects till we're running smoothly.'

She frowned. 'But that doesn't make sense.'

'It does—if you remember that you were running in and out of that bedroom this morning, and I was covering about fifty subjects. You must have walked out in the middle of one, and back in after I'd changed.'

She thought about it. 'But you said something about moving, I know you did——'

He sighed. 'I meant moving into a new production line. Look, if it will make you feel better, I'll take you to Nashville on our honeymoon and introduce you to him.'

'Brett, please don't joke about that any more. You just don't play games like that on the air.'

'Who said it was a game? Just why do you think I showed up on your doorstep this morning?'

Hot colour surged over her face. 'I thought——' she began. 'I never dreamed that you'd come about an apartment. I thought that you were coming to see me——'

'If I'd been trying to avoid you, I certainly wouldn't have come within a mile of your apartment. It's not the only place to live in this town, you know. I was planning to lay siege—rent that apartment and then smoke you out, no matter how long it took. Now that you're going to let me move in with you—you are going to, aren't you? Or shall we wait till the wedding?'

'Brett——' She fended him off. 'You're the one who said it isn't in my nature to be loyal to one man——'

'To Paul,' he corrected. 'There's a difference.' He took a step closer. 'That's why I was furious when I saw that you were still wearing his ring yesterday. Furious, and scared, because I'd played every card I had, and you were still using that diamond like a bit of armour—holding me off, and denying that what was between us was anything special at all. Then I began to fear that perhaps I had imagined it—that you really did love him, and I was nothing to you at all.'

'You were so damned sure of yourself I just wanted to puncture you sometimes——'

'I'm not surprised.' His hands came to rest gently on her shoulders. 'I must have been unbearable.'

'Very nearly.' It was only a whisper, because his touch was enough to make her shiver with anticipation.

'What about it, Rebecca? If you're not sure yet, I understand. We can wait, if you like.'

Wait? she thought. If I have to wait another day, it's more than I can bear!

'But I want you to know that I'm confident that we're meant to be together. You see, I don't believe in love at first sight, but what happened to me was very close. I'd hardly left the studio after the television show that day when I realised how very important it was to me to change your mind, to make you believe in me. And that night, at your father's barbecue, I knew I had to get you away from Paul——'

'You took unfair advantage of me. Making me come up to Chicago——'

'I didn't plan what happened,' he said. 'Forgive me?'

'I do love you,' she said uncertainly.

'You don't have to sound as though you're apologising. Now, may I kiss you, or do you want to argue a little longer first? I always get what I want, eventually, you know. Ask your father; he'll tell you I'm a tough bargainer. If you insist on being difficult, I suppose I could finish ruining your reputation first, but——' The words were light and confident, but his tone held a lingering doubt that made her want to comfort him.

'I'm so crazy about you I'd probably let you do it. And if you've quite made up your mind, there's no point in arguing, is there?' Rebecca asked demurely, and put her arms around him. Her fingertips glided across the softly curling hair at the nape of his neck, and drew his head down to her.

'None at all,' Brett said unsteadily. 'Not when kissing you is so much more fun.' He drew her closer. 'You asked me once why I came back early. I told you the truth, you know. I wanted to see you—to watch your face light up with an idea, to tease you into blushing. That was when I first knew what I'd done—that I'd tripped myself up over a snippy little reporter, and that there would be no peace in my life without you in it.' He looked thoughtfully down at her, and stroked her temples with his thumbs. 'Very likely there won't be much peace with you, either, but— oh, dammit, Rebecca, I love you.'

The door of the broadcast-booth opened, and the receptionist put her head in. 'I'm sorry to interrupt you,' she said, 'but the switchboard is jammed with callers wanting to know what's going on. What should I tell all these people?'

'Tell them they're invited to the wedding,' Brett said unsteadily.

'Somehow,' Janet said drily, 'that doesn't surprise me.'

But neither of them paid any attention to her at all.

NOW ON VIDEO

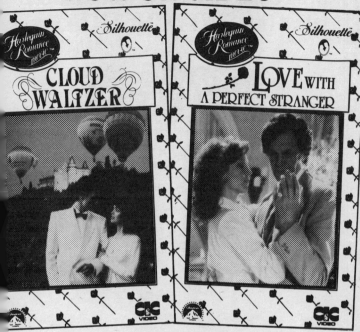

Two great Romances
available on video . . .
from leading
video retailers
for just
£9·99
R.R.P.

The love you find in Dreams.

From Autumn 1987

The 1987 Christmas Pack

Be swept off your feet this Christmas by Charlotte Lamb's WHIRLWIND, or simply curl up by the fireside with LOVE LIES SLEEPING by Catherine George.

Sit back and enjoy Penny Jordan's AN EXPERT TEACHER, but stay on your guard after reading Roberta Leigh's NO MAN'S MISTRESS.

Four new and different stories for you at Christmas from Mills and Boon.

Available in October Price £4.80

Available from Boots, Martins, John Menzies, W. H. Smith, Woolworths and other paperback stockists.

ACCEPT 4
MILLS & BOON
ROMANCES
ABSOLUTELY FREE

...after all, what better way to continue your enjoyment of the finest stories from the world's foremost romantic authors? This is a very special introductory offer designed for regular readers. Once you've read your four **free** books you can take out a subscription (although there's no obligation at all). Subscribers enjoy many special benefits and all these are described overleaf. ►►►

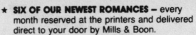